CLA

Pride Publishing books by J.P. Bowie

Single Books
The Set Up
Ride 'em Cowboy
Ride 'em Again Cowboy
Personal Trainers
Halloween Angel
The Officer and the Gentleman
With a Little Help from My Friends
Blood Relations
Nowhere to Hide
Trip of a Lifetime
A Ghost Story
Happy Ending
A Highlander in LA
Journey to Hope
Paris Connection
All I'll Ever Need
Every Breath I Take
Highland Hearts
Evan Sent
Fear and Loving in Las Vegas
Breaking the Habit
Fear of Flying
Love on the Rocks
Murder by Design

The Journeyer
The Journey Begins
The New World
The Fight for Freedom
Into the West

Hot in the Saddle
Vetting the Cowboy

D1447690

My Vampire and I
My Vampire and I
My Vampire Lover
Duet in Blood
Blood Resurrection
Bound in Blood
Blood Lure
Blood Lust
Blood Talisman
Blood Vigilance

Anthologies
Fabulous Brits: Under the Law
Naughty Nooners: Lunches in Laguna
Friction: Cruising
Saddle Up 'N' Ride: Ride 'em Hard Cowboy
Promoted by the Billionaire: Fly to Him
Heatwave: Summer Bliss

Collections
Christmas Spirits: A Present Christmas
Homecoming: Blueprint for Love
Yule Be Mine: A Special Christmas
Immortal Love: Night Wing
A Little Bit Cupid: Valentine's Day Blues

UNBREAK MY HEART

J.P. BOWIE

Unbreak my Heart
ISBN # 978-1-83943-877-6
©Copyright J.P. Bowie 2020
Cover Art by Erin Dameron-Hill ©Copyright April 2020
Interior text design by Claire Siemaszkiewicz
Pride Publishing

This is a work of fiction. All characters, places and events are from the author's imagination and should not be confused with fact. Any resemblance to persons, living or dead, events or places is purely coincidental.

All rights reserved. No part of this publication may be reproduced in any material form, whether by printing, photocopying, scanning or otherwise without the written permission of the publisher, Pride Publishing.

Applications should be addressed in the first instance, in writing, to Pride Publishing. Unauthorised or restricted acts in relation to this publication may result in civil proceedings and/or criminal prosecution.

The author and illustrator have asserted their respective rights under the Copyright Designs and Patents Acts 1988 (as amended) to be identified as the author of this book and illustrator of the artwork.

Published in 2020 by Pride Publishing, United Kingdom.

No part of this book may be reproduced, scanned, or distributed in any printed or electronic form without permission. Please do not participate in or encourage piracy of copyrighted materials in violation of the authors' rights. Purchase only authorised copies.

Pride Publishing is an imprint of Totally Entwined Group Limited.

If you purchased this book without a cover you should be aware that this book is stolen property. It was reported as "unsold and destroyed" to the publisher and neither the author nor the publisher has received any payment for this "stripped book".

UNBREAK MY HEART

London Borough of Hackney	
91300001088195	
Askews & Holts	
AF ROM	£7.49
	6348565

Dedication

What can I say after I say thank you again to Claire and Rebecca at Pride Publishing? Thanks for having enough faith in me that you keep publishing my stories, and thank you, readers, who give me such nice reviews and emails. Oh, and I cannot forget Phil, who frowns if I do— just kidding. Thank you, Phil, for being in my life and making each day one to remember.

Chapter One

Somewhere I read that most people can expect life to deliver a gut punch now and then. Like the time my mom called and told me Dad had emphysema and had to take it easy or else the doctors couldn't guarantee him any kind of longevity. I'd always seen him strong as a horse, unassailable in a way. I wasn't ready to believe he was mortal like the rest of us.

Then there was that moment when everything I'd held dear came crashing down around me. That was when Darren, the love of my life, left me after three years of living and loving — or so I *thought* — together. For the longest time after that trauma it was my complete conviction that no one could ever replace him in looks, ambition or sexual prowess. The many men I've known since then have all seemed the same, with one or two exceptions. Few came close in comparison with the son of a bitch who broke my heart. Not just broke it. Shattered it into tiny bits then stomped on it.

I tried drowning my depression with the aid of booze and in the arms of any random guy who looked at me more than once. But nights of self-indulgence followed by hangovers from hell didn't help soothe the hurt. As each day or week passed, I was more and more certain that the pain of Darren's leaving me without a word, without even a note to tell me he was gone for good, would never really go away.

* * * *

I'd gone to a three-day convention in New York, representing the software company I worked for. The night before I left, we'd had sex. As I'd lingered in the doorway of our apartment clutching my suitcase, he'd kissed me like it was going out of style, as if he'd never see me again. Little did I know. I called him when I got to NYC to let him know I'd arrived safely. I had to leave a message. I called him again before I crashed for the night. Ditto with the message. By morning, when again there was no pickup on his end, I started to worry.

Had something happened to him? An accident of some kind, bad news from his family, a problem at work? None of those things made much sense. Why wouldn't he call to let me know? All morning while I was trying to concentrate on the various convention speakers, thoughts of Darren invaded my mind. At the first break then again at lunchtime and at the end of the day, I called him, but could only leave messages that were beginning to sound slightly frantic.

"Where are you? Has something happened? Call me please, Darren."

"What's up, Jason? You look like you're about to implode." The speaker, William Branson, one of my supervisors at Sonar Electronics, was staring at me, his expression one of amused concern.

"Uh, it's just that I can't get hold of Darren," I told him. "I've called him a dozen times it seems like, and all I get is his voicemail."

"Have you tried his office?"

"He doesn't like me calling him there." I bit my lower lip. Boy, did that sound lame.

William lifted an eyebrow. "He might forgive you this time if something serious has happened."

"Yeah…" *What the hell,* I thought, glancing at my watch. *Almost five.* They didn't close up shop until five-thirty. I punched in his office number on my cell.

"Barker, Hollingworth and Anderson, Attorneys-at-law. This is Cindi. How may I direct your call?"

"Uh, Darren Anderson, please."

"I'm sorry, *Mister* Anderson is not here today."

"What?"

"I said, Mr. Anderson is not here today. Can I take a message?"

"You—you must be mistaken," I sputtered. "Wait, did he call out sick?" A vision of Darren languishing on his bed unable to reach his phone flooded my mind followed immediately by the thought, *That's stupid, if he called out sick, he'd have had to reach his phone.*

"No, sir, he has an out-of-town meeting. May I ask who is calling?"

"Yeah, Jason Harrison. I'm his… I'm a friend." Darren didn't want anyone at the office knowing he was gay and had a live-in lover, me. "A meeting you say? Out of town?" I didn't quite know where to go with this conversation.

"Yes, sir," Cindi replied. I could tell she was trying not to sound as if she was getting impatient. "May I take a message?"

"No, no… I'll try again later."

"Mr. Anderson won't be back in the office until the day after tomorrow, sir."

"What?"

"I said—"

"Yes, I heard what you said. I'm just finding it hard to process. He never mentioned anything about that to me before I left yesterday morning." Oops. Darren would frown heavily if Cindi passed on my concern in that manner. "Uh, I mean, I was on the phone…at the airport."

"Well, Mr. Harrison, I'm sure Mr. Anderson will be happy to return your call when he gets back. Is there anything else I can do for you?"

"No—no, that's okay. Thank you." I hung up and stared bleakly at William who had not moved away but had listened to my end of that entire troubling conversation. He knew about Darren and me and had met Darren on a couple of occasions. "She said he was out of town…at a meeting."

"That's good then. No need to worry. Come on, let's have a drink before dinner."

"It's just strange that he never mentioned any of it to me…the meeting I mean…and going out of town. I don't get it."

"I'm sure there's a rational explanation. It may have just slipped his mind."

I threw him a look of disbelief. "*Darren* letting something like an out-of-town meeting slip his mind? I don't think so."

"Well, try not to worry about it, Jason." He put an arm around my shoulders. "Come on, that bartender looks mighty lonesome over there."

I let him steer me over to the bar and ordered a Scotch rocks when he asked what I wanted. Darren was going to have some explaining to do when I did eventually talk to him.

The convention couldn't end fast enough as far as I was concerned. I'd actually contemplated skipping out early and taking a red-eye back to San Diego, but I knew this would not be viewed amicably by William and my other bosses back at Sonar. William kept trying to assure me that I was worrying needlessly and that when Darren got back to town all would be satisfactorily revealed. On the third day we shared a cab to the airport and I had to listen to him voice his thoughts about how the convention had gone. I couldn't have given a flying fuck on the subject but, somehow, I managed to interject a few thoughts of my own, if only to stop the feelings of dread that kept surfacing in my brain.

William slept through most of the flight back, which was good and bad. Left with only the drone of the plane's engines to fill the silence from my sleeping companion, all kinds of scenarios filled my mind, the overriding one being, of course, that Darren had left me. Hard as that was to imagine or to believe, what other explanation could there be? I had thought of calling his mother, but then nixed the idea for fear of worrying her unduly if she hadn't heard about this 'out-of-town meeting'. Lisa Anderson's health fragile at the best of times and I didn't want to be the one who sent her into a relapse of some kind. Plus, she didn't like me very much, so a call to her would have to be a last resort.

William and I parted ways at the airport and I took a cab for the relatively short ride to our apartment on Sixth Avenue. The concierge gave me a cheery "Good evening, Mr. Harrison" greeting when I rushed past him for the elevators. I figured there would be nothing left of my lower lip if I kept gnashing at it like a nervous rabbit. *Pull yourself together,* I told myself over and over while the elevator climbed to the tenth floor. Like William said, there had to be a rational explanation for this—but what the hell could it be?

Standing outside our apartment door, I took a deep breath, inserted the key in the lock, pushed the door open and stepped inside. The forced jollity of my "Hi, honey, I'm home" died on my lips. It was as if my stomach had sunk to my knees while I stared with horror at the near-empty living room. The bare walls, the missing comfy couch where we'd spent so many evenings cuddling while we watched television—also missing—was hard for me to at first process. My suitcase slipped through my nerveless fingers and dropped with a thud onto the tiled floor. Like a zombie I walked toward the bedroom, already knowing what I'd find. Another near-empty room. The California King bed was gone, along with the nightstands, and the closets on Darren's side were completely bare.

The spare room still had its double bed. Well, at least I wouldn't have to sleep on the floor or find a hotel room for the night. *How thoughtful of you, Darren.* I held back my tears, manfully, and bit back the words of rage that threatened to pour from my mouth. Instead, they screamed at full throttle inside my head.

You've left me, you unmitigated bastard, you soulless son of a bitch. You've left me! I fell to my knees and the dam burst.

The next few weeks sort of passed in a blur of tears, anger and self-recrimination. After all, one has to wonder why, right? My frequent calls to his personal and business numbers went unanswered and that was when the anger surfaced for real. I'm ashamed to admit that I left some pretty horrible messages on his voicemail until the day when I was electronically told that the person I was trying to reach was no longer the owner of the number I had dialed. In addition, when I called his office, I was told in no uncertain terms that Mr. Anderson did not wish to accept my calls.

Okay then. I no longer knew where he lived. I contemplated a face-to-face confrontation in his office, but the coldness of his 'not wishing to take my calls' made me think he might summon security to escort me from the building should I dare to show up unannounced. There was only so much humiliation a guy could take, after all.

The weeks lengthened into months. For a time it seemed as if I were on autopilot. *Get up, go to work, answer when spoken to, go home, stare at the walls while drinking too much Scotch.* Eventually, William called me into his office for a 'chat'.

"Jason…" His expression was one of sympathy mixed with a definite lack of patience. "It's time for you to get over this."

"I'm trying," I mumbled.

"Not hard enough. Look, Jason, I've had complaints from…some people…about you not pulling your weight. They're a bit pissed off with your attitude, which I know is harsh, considering…but this is a place of business, Jason, and we do have a quota to keep up with and... Well, what I'm trying to say, without actually saying it—"

"You're firing me?" I gaped at him, a bit slack-jawed.

"No, not yet, anyway. I don't want to, Jason, you know that. I like you, you're good at what you do, but..."

I sighed, a rush of breath that left me slightly dizzy. I covered my face with my hands. "I'm sorry, William. I'll do better, I promise." I didn't add 'please don't fire me' but I came close. Darren had left me alone to carry the exorbitant rent for the apartment. I'd made a half-assed attempt to find something cheaper, but the last thing I needed was to lose my job. The rent had already punched a giant hole in my savings account.

So pull yourself together, idiot, or join the crowds of the homeless on the streets of San Diego.

I straightened up and met William's gaze full-on. "Sorry about that. I appreciate your concern, William, and I will endeavor to do better from now on."

William nodded and gave me a small smile. "Good. And, Jason, I do know how much Darren has hurt you. Just don't let it ruin your life."

I returned his smile, pretty sure it was more of a grimace than anything else, but it was the best I could do at that moment.

When I got back to the apartment, I looked up the terms of the lease. I was relieved to see that I could give thirty days' notice after six months. We'd been there over a year so...time to get off my ass and *really* look for a cheaper place. I'd miss this address with its beautiful view of the park and easy access to Downtown where I worked, but with the sparse furnishings a constant reminder of Darren's betrayal, I figured it was best that I find somewhere else.

A month later I was living in a one-bedroom apartment in North Park. I bought a new sofa in a completely different style from the one Darren and I had shared, plus some plants and knick-knacks to brighten the living room up. It was quite a cute place and had off-street parking which my Nissan Altima appreciated.

I might sound as if I was in a good state of mind, but that was far from the truth. Despite the shitty way Darren had treated me, I missed him so much that at times it was like a physical ache in my chest. My heart was broken and I was convinced it could never be healed. Not if I lived to be a hundred years old, which at that time I desperately hoped would never happen. Imagine being one hundred and still nursing a broken heart. Okay, common sense, along with my mom and dad and the few friends I had, told me that before I expired, I'd probably get over this.

Why didn't I believe them? Months after Darren had left, I still felt as if I were adrift, unfocused, wandering aimlessly through life…oh, but the self-pity went on and on until even I was sick of myself.

William had told me I needed a night out on the town. He'd even offered to accompany me to a gay bar, which was sweet seeing he wasn't gay. I declined but after a few more weeks of festering and hopelessly longing, I decided maybe that was what I needed. If nothing else, I was getting bored with my empty life of work and watching TV on the new set I'd finally gotten around to buying. I called a friend, Pete Benson, I hadn't seen in a long time.

"Pete, it's Jason Harrison. How are you?"

Pete laughed. "I couldn't believe it when your name popped up on my cell. I'm amazed you still had my number."

"Sorry…yeah, I should've called you sooner."

"Eh, that's okay. I know what it's like when you're in a relationship. His life takes you over kinda. How is Darren?"

"I wouldn't know."

"Oh…bad breakup?"

"You could say that. Listen, I know this is probably crass of me after all this time, but I wondered if you'd like to hang out, go for a drink sometime, maybe?"

"Sometime, maybe?" He chuckled. "How about tomorrow night? I got nothing going on that can't be avoided."

"Tomorrow night's good." I smiled. Something I hadn't done in what seemed like forever.

"Great. Bobby's Tavern? I remember you used to like it there."

He remembered? "Sounds good. Seven-thirty? We can grab something to eat there too. Their tacos were good."

"Still are. Okay, see you tomorrow, Jason. Looking forward to it. We have a lot to catch up on."

As long as he didn't want to talk about shithead Darren. But what were the chances he wouldn't?

* * * *

Bobby's Tavern in Hillcrest, San Diego's Boystown, hadn't changed a bit since the last time I'd been there over two years ago. It hadn't been a favorite of Darren's. He'd thought it was common, so I'd given up on trying to drag him there. Listening to his complaining got to be a bit of a chore after a while.

The noise level hadn't yet reached fever pitch when I got there. That would happen later when the go-go boys appeared and the music was ramped up to an 'are you deaf yet?' level. Pete was already there and he hadn't changed a bit either. Still tall and slender with a shock of blond hair he kept highlighted to perfection. He'd always had a ready smile and that was on full display as I approached.

After we hugged hello, he stepped back and studied me for a moment or two. "You haven't really changed at all. Still beautiful after all these years."

I quirked an eyebrow. "Thanks, flattery will get you anything you want." We laughed together until the good-looking bartender leaned toward us expectantly.

"What'll it be, gents?"

"Uh, Scotch rocks for me," I said. "You, Pete?"

"I think seeing this is a kind of celebration," he said with a whimsical smile, "I will have a vodka martini with olives. I ubered, did you?"

"I did."

"Good boys." The bartender directed a flirty flash of his very white teeth at me. "You can relax and enjoy. Get you something to eat?"

We ordered a plate of tacos each, then once we'd been handed our drinks we retreated to a table by the wall and I braced myself for the inquisition. It didn't take Pete very long.

"So, what happened with you and Darren?"

I took a healthy swig of my Scotch before answering. Or rather trying to answer. It seemed as if the events of the past years that had come crashing to an end with Darren's betrayal smacked me between the eyes anytime someone mentioned his name. The pain in my chest expanded and for a moment I thought it was going to explode.

"I…he…uh…oh shit!" And the tears fell like rain. "Sorry," I blubbed, using the napkin under my glass as a soggy tissue to swipe at my eyes.

"Jason." Pete stared at me, appalled. "Jesus, I'm sorry, sweetie. I had no idea it was still so raw."

"It is, even after all this time, more fool me. He's all I think about, night and day. I can't stop wondering where he is, who he's with, what they're doing, does he ever think of me? On and on." I took another long swig of my Scotch, finishing it off. "Sometimes I think I'm going nuts."

"You're not going nuts, Jason." Pete took my hand and stroked it with his thumb. "And you will get over him eventually. You're a beautiful guy and you need to start looking for someone better than him."

"I'm a beautiful guy?" I knew I sounded bitter.

"Yes, you're a beautiful guy, Jason. I guess you didn't see the reaction from some of the men when you walked in here. You still have the 'it' factor. Don't let this thing with Darren rob you of your self-esteem."

"Then why did he leave me?" I whined. "He found someone more beautiful, more '*it*', or was he just bored and wanted someone new and more exciting?"

Pete sighed. "I don't know all the answers, Jason. But people change. What they thought they wanted they don't want anymore. I know that's not helpful, but if it's any consolation, I think he's a total ass. He obviously didn't appreciate you like he should've. And…and I probably shouldn't say this, but I never liked him. Way too full of himself."

A young guy appeared at our table at that moment, carrying enormous plates of tacos which he set in front of us. "Hot sauce?"

"Please," Pete said, tipping the guy.

I stared at the delicious-smelling food and was suddenly not at all hungry.

"Eat up." Pete dug in immediately.

"I need another drink," I muttered and started to get up.

Pete put a hand on my arm. "I'll get 'em this time. Go on, start eating."

I sat back down and lifted a taco to my mouth, nibbling at the fragrant meat. Okay, it was great and I really should eat something if I was going to have more than one drink.

"Got you a double," Pete said, sitting by me. "Oh good, you're eating." He laughed. "God, I sound like a mother hen or something." He raised his glass to mine. "It's really good to see you, Jason. Don't wait so long next time."

We clinked glasses and I said, "I won't," around a mouthful of taco. Was it the ambience of Bobby's Tavern, Pete's good-natured company, or the booze that was giving me a distinctly warm glow inside? I sat back and gazed around the bar, at the guys in groups and singles, shooting the breeze or just looking…for what? A quick fuck, or something more…companionship. *I used to have that,* I thought. *I used to think it would last forever.* The glow faded. I threw my drink back, lurched to my feet and headed for the bar.

"Whoa, Jason." Pete was at my side. "Slow down. You don't want to get hammered so fast."

"I'm fine. You joining me or what?"

"Just get me a soda. I have to work tomorrow."

I nodded, ordered myself a double and a soda for Pete. The bartender grinned. "Whatcha doing later?"

"You, if I'm not mistaken."

His grin got wider and his eyes narrowed to feral slits. "You're not mistaken. Get rid of your friend. I get off early tonight."

"Best news of the week," I told him.

Chapter Two

I woke next morning with a throbbing head and a sore ass. I lay alone in my bed and tried to piece together the events of the previous evening. After Pete had failed to persuade me to leave, he'd kissed me goodnight and left the bar after eliciting a promise from me that I'd call him and tell him I got home okay. Had I called him? Hadn't a clue. I'd had a couple more drinks. I shouldn't have but it'd seemed like a good idea at the time. The bartender...what was his name again? Mark or Matt or something. I remembered him all right. He'd driven me home. I must've asked him in 'cause I had the distinct impression that he'd been here last night. In my bed, in my mouth and definitely in my ass. Hence, the still raw ache as if I'd been fucked many times over.

Shit. I hope we used condoms. The sheets were a mess of dry cum and lube streaks. I got up to use the bathroom and breathed a sigh of relief when I saw the evidence of safe sex I was hoping for. I washed my hands and stared at my reflection in the mirror. Pete had said I still looked beautiful. I've always found it hard to think of myself that way. Yeah, I have thick dark hair that's easy to keep from getting unruly, blue eyes Darren used to call 'bewitching' and say he could gaze into them forever. *Okay, don't go there.* I've kept up working out even on my most depressing day so the bod's still okay, but on closer inspection I could see the start of fine lines around those *bewitching* eyes. To be expected, I suppose, as I approached thirty.

Coffee.

I staggered into the kitchen and much to my surprise there was a note propped against the already prepped coffee maker. I picked up the note and flipped the on switch at the same time.

Jason, thanks. You were terrific. If you want another round, you know where I work. Matt.

Mystery solved. His name was Matt—and I was terrific. Good to know, because I had only the haziest memory of hot flesh pressed to mine, wet kisses and a burning sensation the first time he'd fucked me. Had I enjoyed it as much as he had?

Hadn't a clue. Which reminded me. I scanned the living room and spied my crumpled jeans in a far corner. *My, we must have been in a hurry.* I found my cell in my jeans back pocket and punched in Pete's number. It went to voicemail of course. He'd told me he had to work today. I did remember that.

"Hey, Pete, sorry it took me so long to let you know I got home safe and sound. Give me a call when you're up to it."

I slumped onto the couch and waited for the coffee to brew. Now that the events of last night had come into focus, I wasn't very pleased with myself. It had been years since I'd had drunken sex. College days. Meeting Darren and falling in love with him had ensured that I at least had been monogamous for the three years we'd been together. We'd even stopped using condoms. Having sex with anyone other than Darren had never even crossed my mind. Obviously, I'd been on my own with that vow of fidelity. The coffee maker pinged and I got up to pour a much-needed mug of the hot brew. It was Saturday, the day I did laundry and checked in with my folks. Jeez, all this excitement was gonna kill me.

Saturdays used to be Darren and me strolling through Farmer's Market, a picnic lunch in the park or maybe a drive down to the beach, dinner with friends at night or sometimes just a lazy day where we would kick back and ignore our phones. We both worked hard and a day of nothing but spending time together, a lot of it in bed making slow and tender love, was, for me, Nirvana. Now I wasn't sure what it had been for Darren. Was he even then thinking of how he was going to leave me? How long had he been formulating that plan to just move out without a word? And why? What had I done, or not done, that was so terrible he couldn't leave a note with the reason for his departure?

Five months later and I still didn't know. In the circle of our friends there were some who definitely had been more Darren's friends than mine. Not one of them had returned any of my calls. Loyalty to Darren or just an expression of dislike for loser me? My friends, the ones I'd known before hooking up with Darren, said they didn't know the reason, that on the few occasions we'd all got together, Darren had never intimated he was out of love with me. And some, like Pete, didn't even know we'd split.

I finished my mug and poured another. My phone chimed and I glanced at the screen. *Mom*. Shit, I'd left it just a little too late for the regular time she had made me promise I'd call by. So she could stop worrying about me, she'd said.

"Hi, Mom."

"Jason, is everything all right? You usually call before this time on a Saturday. Are you sick?"

"No, just a little hungover. I met with a friend last night and I guess I'm not used to having more than one or two drinks. It was a late night and I slept in. Just having my coffee now. How are you?"

"Oh, Jason, were you drinking because of *him*?" she asked, avoiding my attempt to change the subject.

"No, Mom. I just needed a night out, so I called Pete. Remember him?"

"Oh yes, sweet boy. How is he?"

Sweet boy. He and I are almost thirty. "He's fine. It was good seeing him again. So what's new with you and Dad?"

We spent the next twenty minutes talking about my dad's health and what he wasn't doing to please the doctor. Dad had emphysema but wouldn't give up on his gardening, which the doc said put a strain on his heart.

"By the way, it's his birthday in two weeks and we'd like you to come up and celebrate with us. You can stay the night so you won't have to make the drive afterward."

My parents live in Sherman Oaks, which is a couple of hours from San Diego on a good traffic day.

"We thought we'd have a dinner on Saturday with some friends and you…and if there's anyone you'd like to bring?"

"That would be no one, Mom, but thanks for the thought."

"All right. Why don't you come up early in the afternoon so we can spend some time before the others get here?"

"Sounds good, Mom. I'll see you then. Give Dad a hug for me."

After we hung up, I thought, and not for the first time, just how lucky I was to have such great parents. They'd been supportive of me all my life. Darren's mom and dad hadn't liked the fact that he was gay. They hadn't thrown him out, but there had been a definite chill in the air when he and I had visited them. It was surprising to me because Darren was so handsome and successful. Things they should have been proud of, but much too often bigotry negates parental pride.

I wandered into the bedroom and pulled the sheets off the bed, sticking them in the laundry basket after then finding clean ones from the linen closet. The phone rang just as I was attempting 'hospital corners' on the top sheet. Darren had insisted on those, and old habits die hard, it seemed.

"Hey, Pete. Did you get my message?"

"Yeah. Glad you made it home okay."

"Matt, the bartender, drove me."

"I figured. He was fucking you with his eyes the whole time I was there. Did you get lucky?"

"I guess so. To be honest I don't remember much about it, but my ass reminds me every now and then."

Pete chuckled. "I could say it was just what you needed, but you'd know that better than me."

"You wanna go back there tonight?"

"I can't, sorry. I have a date."

"Oh yeah? Do I know him?"

"Probably not. I just met him last week. He's from Portland, Oregon. Nice guy."

"Well, you have fun. Be in touch, okay?"

I hung up and went back to finish making the bed, a vague feeling of envy mixed with disappointment clouding my brain. It would've been nice to go out again...two nights in a row, oh boy. Of course, there was no reason why I couldn't go on my own. That'd be different...and just a bit scary. Which was ridiculous. And Matt the bartender would be there. Maybe he'd be up for another round. Or was I going to look desperate showing up so soon? Or would he be flattered? Only one way to find out, but right then, the laundry room called.

The rest of the day while I finished the laundry, cleaned the apartment, went grocery shopping, I dithered about whether to go back to Bobby's Tavern or spend the night at home with a frozen pizza and Netflix. *Come on,* I told myself, *you've spent way too many nights at home already these past months. Trekking up to Sherman Oaks to see Mom and Dad, or going for a drink with William now and then does not constitute a rip-roaring social life. Go out, have a drink, have fun and maybe get laid. Sounds like a plan.*

* * * *

Saturday night and Bobby's Tavern was jumping when I got there around eight. I thought it might have still been quiet enough for me to make my presence known to Matt and maybe get some idea if he wanted to play again. No such luck. Apart from the place being packed, there was no sign of Matt. There were two bartenders working, shirtless and hot, but no Matt. When I finally managed to inch my way to the bar counter, I ordered a Scotch and asked the bartender, while trying not to stare too hard at his massive pecs, if Matt was around.

"He's off tonight," he yelled over the noise of the other patrons.

"Oh, okay, thanks." I grabbed my drink and pushed my way out of the three-deep press of bodies over to the dance floor where there was at least at two-foot space to stand in. No Matt. Well that was a bummer, but I was out and the eye-candy was plentiful on the dance floor. Some pretty, lithe bodies, stripped down to their jeans, slid sinuously together, the bulges at fly level telling me they had no time for anything or anyone else.

A tap on the shoulder had me turning around and coming face to face and almost chest to chest with a nice-looking older guy. He was slightly taller than my six-feet, blond hair silvering at the temples, blue eyes and a great smile.

"Would you care to dance?" he asked.

"How can I resist such good manners?" I replied, grinning. I swallowed what was left of my drink, placed the glass on the edge of the bar and followed him onto the floor. "I'm Jason," I said, stepping into the circle of his arms.

"Kelly Atherton. I haven't seen you here before."

"I was here last night. The first time in years. You're a regular?" I had thankfully avoided the old clichéd 'You come here often?'

"Not really. Couple of times a month when I'm in town."

"Oh, you're not from here then." *You're so quick, Jason.*

"Los Angeles... Pasadena actually."

"My folks live in Sherman Oaks."

"Nice."

The music's slightly frantic pace slowed to a dreamier tempo and before I really knew what I was doing, I had dropped my head on his shoulder, and was nuzzling his neck. He tightened his arms around me and there was no mistaking the hardness behind his fly. Nice to know I could still turn someone on that fast. After all, Matt had said I was terrific. Too bad I couldn't remember just how terrific I'd been. I chuckled softly to myself at my own silliness.

Kelly raised his head to gaze at me. His blue eyes really were beautiful. "What's so funny?"

"I was just remembering something someone said. Nothing important."

His lips quirked and I wanted to kiss them, so I did. He kissed me back, his lips warm and soft and when I opened for him, he slipped his tongue over mine, sending a tingling sensation down my spine straight to my balls.

"Would you like to take this further?" he murmured when we unlocked our lips.

"You ask so nicely, how can I refuse?"

* * * *

So for the second time in two nights I had sex with a stranger. What had I been thinking? Not much beyond the sex which, disappointingly, wasn't that great. Kelly was a sweet guy, but there was no passion in what we did, at least from my perspective. Maybe I was expecting too much or maybe I was too sober. There just didn't seem to be much of a connection, and I was glad we'd gone back to his hotel room so I could leave gracefully.

"I'll be back in town next month," he said as I kissed him goodbye on the cheek.

"Great. Give me a call." We'd swapped numbers earlier on the way over to his hotel. I called for an Uber and, as I waited outside for it to show up, I felt deflated. Not how I expected to feel after sex, even mediocre sex. Truth was I'd been spoiled by Darren. No matter his lack of morals and loyalty, the guy had been dynamite in bed and I suspected it would be difficult to find someone who could come close to his prowess. I wished I could really remember more of my time with Matt. Had he been good? Only one way to find out, I told myself. Tomorrow night I would go back to the bar and find out if he was interested in another 'round' like he'd suggested.

The Uber driver showed up and I climbed in. I stared at the back of his head as he pulled away from the curb. He had nice curly black hair and his voice as he asked me if I'd had a good evening was deep and mellow.

"Somewhat disappointing," I replied.

"Oh?" He did a slight turn of his head and I caught a glimpse of his profile. His strong nose and chin were enough to interest me and I leaned forward to close the distance between us. What was I doing? It seemed to me that since finally breaking down and having sex with Matt it was all I could think of. Sex, and the craving to have more. I told myself to cool it. I'd just been laid for goodness sake, but it didn't seem like enough. The urge to touch the back of the driver's neck was almost overwhelming.

"Disappointing in what way?" he asked, picking up our conversation.

"Uh, the company I was in, I guess," I said, sitting back and again telling myself to get a grip.

"Been there, done that… I'm Joey by the way." He did a half-turn again and I got a second shot at admiring his profile. Was he Italian or Greek descent? Whatever, he was hot.

"Jason. Nice to meet you."

"So, you have other plans for the evening?"

"It's getting late, so probably not." I got a surprise when he pulled over to the side of the road then turned to look at me. Even in the murkiness of the car's interior I could tell he was handsome. He reached over, grabbed my coat and pulled me forward. Our mouths clashed together and I winced slightly as my lips felt like they'd been bruised by the collision.

What the…? Shocked, I opened my mouth to protest and he slid his tongue inside and, just like that, I gave in to its sensual glide and the tingling sensation of his lips over mine.

"Jesus," I whispered when he released me. "How did you know I'd enjoy that?"

He grinned. "You know what they say, it takes one to know one." He kissed me again, and again. I groaned and slipped my arms around his neck and shoulders.

"This seat is most definitely in the way," I told him, my voice no more than a croak.

"Your place then? You're my last ride for the night."

"Maybe not quite your last," I said and he chuckled at my cheesy remark.

Later, I would wonder at the craziness of my actions. A guy I'd known for less than ten minutes and I was going to let him fuck me, or me him. I wasn't sure which it would be, but I was all up for it, give or take, in more ways than one. I was hard as a rock, regardless of just having had sex less than an hour ago. My life had taken a definite sharp turn, but for good or for bad, I guess I was going to find out.

Chapter Three

Joey liked to kiss and he was good at it. Not as good as Darren but I really had to stop comparing other men to the guy who'd dumped me. *Just enjoy the moment,* I told myself when Joey pressed me against the entryway wall and started to undress me, raining kisses on my chest once he'd unbuttoned my shirt. He dropped to his knees and unzipped me, murmuring with what sounded like approval when my cock sprang out to meet his lips. He kneaded my ass cheeks and pulled me in closer, swallowing me whole. I ran my hands through his curls and pumped slowly in and out of his mouth. He was good at this too, using his tongue to great effect and bringing me to the brink almost too quickly.

Hauling him to his feet, I suggested we get naked and get on the bed. He agreed happily and asked where I kept the lube and condoms. He fucked me and made me come then left with a promise to give me a call. After I'd shut the door behind him, I went back to bed and lay staring up at the ceiling for what seemed like an eternity, unable to sleep despite my two bouts of sex. Joey had been better than Kelly but still not terrific, although I'd known he'd been trying very hard to please me. When he'd asked if I was still disappointed, I'd smiled and told him no. An easy lie so as not to hurt his feelings.

I had determined to live up to my promise to William to drop the attitude and pull my weight at work, thus avoiding the hostile looks from the rest of the staff and securing my position there. So far so good, and I took on a project with Hank Stevens, one of my colleagues, that William wanted done yesterday, or so he said.

"This client is a stickler for things being completed on time, so, guys, give it a hundred percent, okay?"

Hank and I both nodded and got to work. At lunchtime, Hank asked if I like to grab a sandwich with him.

"I like the deli on the corner," he said. "How about you?"

"That's good." I gave him a quick smile, surprised by his suggestion. We'd never had lunch together, but I had noticed that the two he'd palled around with previously hadn't seemed quite so friendly toward him. Being all caught up in my own misery, I hadn't thought to ask what the problem was but, on our way out, I noticed one of his ex-buddies giving us both a dirty look. So, of course, I had to ask.

After we'd found a window table at Frank's Deli, I popped the question...well, not that question, obviously. "What's with John and Phil? I caught that sneer from John when we were leaving."

Hank sighed. "I stupidly came out to them a couple of weeks ago. I thought they'd be okay with it, but they weren't and now they snub me at every turn and throw snide remarks when no one's around."

I grimaced. "Did you mention it to William? He won't stand for that kind of crap."

"I don't want to stir anything up."

"But you shouldn't have to put up with it in the workplace. This is California, not Alabama. He can just remind them of company policy at the next office meeting."

He smiled sadly. "Thanks for being so supportive, Jason. You want to go out with me for a drink some night?"

I blinked. I hadn't expected that. Hank was good-looking in an unassuming way. Brown hair, brown eyes, a small mouth. Just not my type, but it wouldn't be any skin off my nose to go out for a drink with him…cheer him up a little. Maybe even make me feel better about myself.

"It won't be a date, or anything like that," he added quickly. "I wouldn't presume…" He tapered off and squirmed a little on his seat.

"Okay," I said, meeting his sad eyes. "What about Thursday? You pick the place."

Hank looked surprised and relieved at the same time. Maybe he'd been bracing for a rejection, so I was glad I'd said yes. Another snub on top of John and Phil's might have been enough to send him into a fit of depression. We chatted about this and that for the rest of the lunchbreak and it wasn't until we were back in the office that I realized he hadn't asked about my breakup with Darren…nor had I thought about my ex for a whole hour. Was this some kind of breakthrough?

For the rest of the day, we were busy finishing up the project William had given us and when we brought our blueprint to him just before five, I thought he was going to kiss us both. "You guys are the greatest," he crowed, beaming at us. "I knew I'd given this to the right people." I glanced through his office window at John and Phil's glowering faces. They'd obviously heard William's words of praise. He did tend to get loud when he was excited about something. I loitered in William's office after Hank went back to his desk.

"Can I have a word?"

"Sure, close the door and take a seat." William was full of bonhomie. "Good to see you back in form, Jason. You over that jerk leaving you?"

"Not really, but that's not what I want to talk to you about."

"You're not thinking of quitting, are you?"

I chuckled at his somber expression. "No. It's about Hank. He told me at lunch today that a couple of guys in the office are giving him the cold shoulder and directing shitty remarks at him since he came out to them."

William smirked. "He had to come out to them? What are they, deaf and blind?"

"No, just assholes. Not everyone's as observant as you. But they have to know they shouldn't be doing any of that shit here in the office. I'd like you to stress that point at the next meeting."

"Who are they?"

"I'd rather not say. They might make it even tougher for Hank if you confront them."

"Fuck. I can't believe we still have that problem in this day and age. You know me, Jason, I hate racists and homophobes and I don't want any of them working for me."

I nodded. "And I love you for it, but let's not make a big deal about it. If they back off from the snide remarks after you remind everyone of our zero-tolerance policy, that'll help Hank a lot. I don't think he's interested in being buddies with them again, just wants a friendly atmosphere at work."

"Buddies, huh?" William looked as if he'd solved the secrets of the universe. "Now I know who you're talking about. Okay, I won't single them out, but they'll know that I know who they are."

I grinned. "Make 'em squirm some. That'll be enough."

"It'd better be, otherwise it's the door."

* * * *

Halfway through the week I had a definite itch that I needed someone to scratch so I decided to pay Bobby's Tavern a visit just to see if Matt might be there. It seemed that although I'd already had sex with three different men, it still wasn't enough. What was I going to do—keep on fucking until I found the one who could satisfy me like Darren had? In my mind there wasn't a whole lot wrong with that idea, although I wondered if I had the stamina for it.

Matt was behind the bar when I entered Bobby's Tavern. He gave me a flirtatious smile and a wave and I was pretty sure it was meant to indicate he was ready for another 'round' with me.

"Hey, beautiful, what'll it be tonight?"

"The usual, Scotch on the rocks. How've you been?"

"Good."

I watched while he quickly made my drink then placed it in front of me, holding the glass just long enough for our fingertips to touch as I reached for it.

"Are you off early again tonight?" I asked.

"It could be arranged," he replied with a sly smile.

"Arrange it then. This time I'd like to remember more of what we did."

He chuckled. "You were pretty hammered, but you were really *flexible*." He disappeared at that moment to answer a customer's call for service and I leaned on the bar, surveying the other guys standing around. Why was it that when I looked at other guys, all I could do was compare them with Darren? Why did I continue to torture myself by imagining us reconciled and declaring vows of undying love...again?

Now that I was out in the public domain once more, there was a chance we might bump into each other. San Diego is a fairly big city but not so big that one could never come face to face with someone from the past. Would I be horrified, or melt into a puddle of goo at the sight of him? I knew that, impossible as it was, I longed for his arms around me, his lips on mine thrilling me like no other man ever had or, it seemed, ever would.

I wandered over to the bar and ordered another Scotch rocks. Matt leaned close and whispered, "A half-hour. Are you ready for me?"

I nodded. "You bet." But I had to admit that a little of the fire I'd felt earlier had diminished. However, I wasn't going to renege on Matt. I needed someone to hold me, to make me forget, if for just an hour or two, everything Darren. Even though I knew it was improbable, I was going to have a damned good try.

By the time Matt stood in front of my table in all his arrogant sexiness, I was nicely buzzed, but far from drunk. I was going to remember this night with Matt and hoped like hell it would be everything I had imagined and hoped it would be.

* * * *

Like Joey the driver, Matt wasted no time in slamming me up against the wall and ripping my shirt open. His cock was already hard when he pressed against me and his lips were hot when he scoured my chest and roughly teased my nipples. He was an eager lover and I was determined to make the most of his prowess. I grabbed the hem of his T-shirt and yanked it up and over his head. Our bare chests slapped together and I forced my mouth on his, thrilled when his lips parted and our tongues tangled. We writhed against each other, sliding our hands over each other's torsos with fevered caresses.

"Bed," I murmured in his ear and he grabbed me by the hand and practically raced to the bedroom. Like I said, an eager lover. We stripped each other of what remained of our clothes, jeans, briefs and shoes, and I stepped back to get a load of Matt's tasty physique. I remembered from that first night in the bar when he'd stood shirtless in front of me that he had a hot body, but seeing him again up close was a feast for the eyes. He was my height, but his shoulders were wider and his chest hairier, his torso tapering down to slim hips and muscular thighs. The right stuff.

"You really are a wonderful sight to behold," I told him.

Grinning, he tossed me onto the bed and climbed on top of me, trailing kisses from my lips down to my groin, running his tongue over the head of my dick before taking it all with one long swallow. I arched into him and his throat muscles clenched around my cock, and I saw stars. Yeah, he was good all right. I ran my fingers through his thick dark hair. He moaned then, with a practiced move, shifted around so that his glistening shaft hovered over my mouth. I licked at the pre-cum pooling around the slit. He tasted as good as he looked and, searching for more, I took all of him down to the base.

He shuddered over me and picked up the pace of his sucking, at the same time massaging my balls and perineum, fingering my hole. He wanted to fuck me and I was going to let him. All I remembered from our last time was my aching ass. Now I wanted to experience the whole thing totally sober. I flopped over onto my side and dragged him on top of me.

"Fuck me," I told him.

"You got it," he muttered and reached for the nightstand drawer which I had refilled the day before. I yelped when the cold lube hit my anus and he laughed when I wiggled my ass at him impatiently. "You're ready for me, aren't you?"

Dumb question. There I was with my legs in the air, asshole exposed — I couldn't be more ready if I tried. He breached me and slid his long cock all the way in. Just as well I was no virgin. It still burned, but the discomfort soon faded and his slow rhythmic pass over my prostate was like heaven.

"Oh yeah," I sighed on a breath. "Right there, Matt. Right. Fucking. There."

He grinned down at me. "So fucking sexy," he growled then bent to take my lips with his in a scorching kiss that dizzied me. I wrapped my arms around his neck and deepened the kiss, scouring the inside of his mouth with my tongue which he met with his own, tangling and twisting them together until we were both panting into each other's mouths.

He rammed into me and I howled my rapture. He was good, oh so good. I clung to him, my arms and legs holding him fast while he plunged deep inside me again and again. He reared back, muscles straining, his face contorted with ecstasy. Sweat dropped from his forehead onto my lips and I licked it up, savoring the saltiness. He gripped my erection and began pumping it in time to his own quickening rhythm.

"Matt," I groaned.

"Yeah, babe…come on. I'm close, come with me…"

I came first, unable to hold back the wrenching cry of release, cum surging from me and splattering over my chest and chin. Matt's eyes were shut tight, his lips pulled back to bare his teeth, and a sound very much like a growl escaped him. His body stiffened over me and the heat of his semen as he filled the condom seated deep within me was an unexpected thrill. He collapsed over me, our sweaty bodies heaving. He trailed his lips over my face until he found my mouth and we traded wet, breathy kisses while we recovered.

"Oh man," he whispered after a while. "You are one hot fuck."

I chuckled weakly. "Not the most romantic thing I've ever heard, but I'll take the compliment."

"Oh, I can do romance if you want," Matt said, nuzzling my ear, "but I got the feeling you were in it just for the sex."

"I am. No more relationships for me. Once burned, as they say."

"Know what you mean. So, you wanna be fuck buddies with me?"

"Is that still a thing?" I asked, pinching his left nipple.

He grabbed my hand and pulled me in for a kiss. "It's still a thing, and I think we'd be good at it."

"Okay."

He rolled off the bed and headed for the bathroom muttering something about getting rid of the condom. I lay back and thought about what he'd said. *Fuck buddies*. I'd never been one before, but it had a satisfactory ring to it. Sex without commitment. No worries if Matt saw someone else or if I met a guy who got my juices going. This might just be the answer to my depression, having as much sex as possible, that is.

I could only hope.

Chapter Four

Hank had chosen The Gallery, a nice little gay bar on University for our 'not a date'. He showed up just after I got there. We'd decided to run home first and change into something more suitable for a night out and he looked so different in a pair of skinny jeans and a blue short-sleeved shirt that nicely displayed his biceps I'd never noticed before.

"You look nice," I said when he joined me at the bar.

"So do you, but then you always do."

"Flatterer." I chuckled. "What'll you have?"

"Stella on tap, please."

I ordered for him and a Scotch rocks, my favorite drink, for me. We carried our drinks over to a nearby table and sat facing each other.

"This is great," he said, looking around at the other patrons. "I never do this."

"Never?"

"Well, hardly ever. When John and Phil were still talking to me, we'd go out for a drink sometimes but always to straight bars of course."

I frowned. "You don't have other friends…gay friends?"

He shook his head. "I'm bad at communicating with people." He smiled shyly. "You have no idea how much it took to ask you to lunch, never mind if you'd go out with me for a drink."

"But you did, and it wasn't that hard, was it?"

"I really expected you to say no."

"Why? Am I that unapproachable?"

"Well, you're so good-looking and I…" He glanced away toward the far end of the bar and when he faced me again, he'd gone decidedly pale. "You'll never guess who's sitting at the bar down there."

"Someone we know?" I turned and stared at the back of a familiar figure deep in conversation with another guy. "Fuck me," I muttered.

"It is him, isn't it?" Hank whispered. "I'm not mistaken."

"No, you're not mistaken. It's John all right. That fucking hypocrite." I stood but Hank grabbed my wrist.

"Don't say anything to cause a scene, Jason."

"I won't cause a scene. I just want him to know his cover's been blown and he'd better apologize to you for the shit he's been giving you."

"Okay, but let's not do it here. He's going to be humiliated enough when we tell him we know."

I grinned at him and sat back down. "You are spoiling my fun, Hank. I so wanted to see the look on his face when I tapped him on the shoulder and said hi!"

He grinned back at me then swallowed the last of his beer. "Let's go someplace else. I don't think I can stomach seeing him in here."

"Okay. Bobby's Tavern is just down the road. We can go there."

A very different place from The Gallery, Bobby's Tavern was jumping as usual when we arrived. Hank immediately went into shy mode, sticking so close to my side we might have been conjoined twins. Matt wasn't on duty, but his replacement was a cute guy who told us his name was Brett. I shook his hand and introduced Hank who looked both terrified and intrigued by Brett's expansive personality. If I'd have been on my own, I might have been tempted to flirt and even ask what time he got off. After all, I'd vowed to have as much sex as possible.

I controlled myself. I did have Hank here to kind of look after. He might panic if I left him on his own with so many hot guys pressing in on us from all sides. He bought this round and we carefully pushed our way through the madding crowd toward the dance floor.

"There's a bit more space up ahead," I told Hank and he grabbed the hem of my T-shirt, I presumed so we wouldn't get separated. We'd no sooner got to the dance floor when some big guy threw his arm around Hank's waist and, with an excited "Wanna dance?", hauled him away from me. I just managed to grab his drink before he disappeared into the mob, my last glimpse of him his startled, bug-eyed expression. I chuckled and told myself this was what he needed. At least he didn't cry for help.

I leaned my back against the bar and watched the gyrations going on in front of me. Some hot guys for sure. San Diego has great eye-candy. Two guys, hot and sweaty, extracted themselves from the press. One I recognized, my friend Pete. He looked flushed and happy. His partner, a tall black dude, kept a possessive arm around him as they approached me.

"Jason! You here on your own?"

"No, with a guy from the office. He's in there somewhere." I indicated the crowd of dancing queens.

"This is Brandon," he said, nudging the guy who stuck out his hand.

"Hi, Brandon."

"Hi." He started to drag Pete back onto the dance floor, but Pete wasn't having it.

"I'm done."

"Oh, come on, man," Brandon whined. "This is my last night here."

Pete rolled his eyes and sighed. "You gonna be here for a while?" he asked me.

"Yeah. At least until Hank shows up, hopefully in good working order. He doesn't get out to places like this very much."

Pete laughed. "Okay, maybe see you later." And they were gone.

I downed my Scotch and signaled at Brett for a refill. While I waited, I glanced down the length of the bar and froze. *Fuck me, if it isn't that asshole John in here with some guy. Probably the one he was talking to at The Gallery.*

Okay, I couldn't resist. I sidled down to where he was standing with his friend, tapped him on the shoulder and said, "Hi, John, fancy seeing you here."

He turned, looked me up and down and smiled. "You must think I'm my brother. My name is Spencer, but it's an easy mistake. John is my twin. And you are?"

"Totally embarrassed."

Spencer laughed and held out his hand which I shook gladly. "I'm Jason. I work with your brother."

"Poor you. This is my husband, Cary."

We shook hands and exchanged pleasantries which was no mean feat with the blaring music and excited chatter surrounding us. I gathered Spencer and Cary lived in Denver and were here in San Diego for a long weekend.

"Are you seeing John?" I asked.

"Not if I can help it. He's the biggest downer of all time. I didn't tell him we were going to be here." He studied me for a moment then said, "I bet you couldn't believe your eyes when you thought it was John standing in the middle of a gay bar."

"You're right. He's quite the homophobe. Oh, and here comes Hank, another colleague of John's."

A shirtless Hank's happy expression morphed into one of horror as he hesitantly approached us. He said something to his dance partner who put a proprietary arm around his shoulders and hugged him close. I figured I'd better say something quick.

"Don't worry, it's not John. Spencer is his twin brother, and this is his husband, Cary."

"Oh." Hank managed a smile and we stood among the jostling crowd exchanging introductions. Hank's new friend was Lewis and now that I could get a good look at him, I could see he was ruggedly handsome with brown eyes and light brown hair cut really short. *A marine,* I guessed, *or maybe navy SEAL.* Score one for Hank who was smiling like he'd found gold.

It was impossible to get into an in-depth conversation surrounded by guys and some women all trying to drown out the music with their yelling. I'd had enough and now that Hank was suitably hooked up, I was ready to go. I bid everyone goodnight and left the noise and crazy ambience behind. I pulled out my phone to summon Uber service.

What were the chances? Joey's smiling face beamed at me when he pulled his car in front of Bobby's Tavern.

"How'd you do that?" I asked, climbing in beside him.

He squeezed my thigh and grinned. "Just dumb luck I guess."

"Am I your last ride for the night?"

"No, but I can cut out for an hour or so if you like."

"I like. Home, Joey, and make it snappy."

* * * *

Naturally I wanted all the good news from Hank the next morning. He had a glow about him that didn't come from spending the night alone.

"He's fantastic," he whispered in response to my nosiness as we stood by the office coffee maker.

"Did you do it?"

Hank's face flushed adorably at my teasing remark. "He said he didn't do that on a first meeting, but he wants to see me again."

"Wow, a gentleman," I said, thinking of my own lack of restraint with the last three guys I'd met. "Good for him. When are you seeing him again?"

"Tonight!"

"That's great, Hank. I'm happy for you."

"And I have you to thank for taking me to that bar. I'd never have dared go there by myself."

"So, a whole new world has opened up for you. Enjoy, my friend, and ignore the assholes, one of whom is heading our way even as we speak."

"Shit," Hank muttered.

John sneered something like 'pansies' when he brushed by us and poured himself a cup of coffee.

"Hey, John…" I made sure I was loud enough for most people to hear. "We ran into your twin brother and his *husband* last night at Bobby's Tavern. He said to not say 'hi' to you." John just stood staring at me, so I plowed on. "Hard to believe he's your brother…such a charming guy. How come you didn't tell us you had a gay twin brother?"

"I *don't* have a gay twin brother. He's been dead to me ever since he came out ten years ago."

"Dead to you?" I stared at him with wide eyes. "What kind of antediluvian crap is that? This is the twenty-first century, John, not the Dark Ages."

"It's also none of your fucking business," John snarled.

"You're right," I said. "However, it is my business, and everyone else's in this office, when you start harassing members of our team because you don't like the fact that they are gay."

"Okay, Jason…" William strode toward us, his expression grim. "I'll handle this. Everyone back to your desks."

Dutifully we did as he'd instructed.

"This actually was going to be the opening subject of our meeting today," William said. "I thought it was understood that there is a rule of zero tolerance with regard to abuse because of religion, gender, race or sexual orientation within the workplace. Harassment of any kind will not be tolerated here at Sonar. It has come to my attention that there have been incidents of such behavior, and I will not stand for it. Is that understood? Anyone found giving another member of our team a bad time for any reason without first coming to me with their complaint will be terminated. Okay, now that we've got that cleared up, let's get on to other matters…"

After the meeting William asked John and Phil to join him in his office. Hank sent me a look that I interpreted as thanks. After a few minutes John and Phil marched out of William's office and back to their desks, rather pointedly avoiding either my or Hank's eyes.

At lunch, Hank told me he and Lewis had danced the night away after I'd left then Lewis had driven him home, and they'd made out in the car. "He's a fantastic kisser. I asked him to come up, but he said next time. Like I told you, he said he doesn't go the whole way the first time he's with a guy. I just hope there'll be a next time."

"I'm sure of it," I told him. "I saw the way he was looking at you."

"Well, he has my phone number so it's up to him."

"You don't have his number?"

"Oh, well, yeah…" Hank blushed. "I just don't want to seem pushy."

"Seem *interested*, Hank. That's not being pushy."

"You think?"

"I know. When was the last time you had a boyfriend?"

"Ages. When I was twenty-one."

"And you are now?"

"Twenty-four."

"Not ages, then, but it's definitely time for you to have another one, and Lewis might just be the one."

Hank finished his sandwich and patted his mouth with his napkin. "What about you? Don't you want a boyfriend?"

"I had one and he left me." God, how much it hurt to say that, even after all this time. "So, I'm playing the field as they say. I have a fuck buddy."

Hank wrinkled his nose. "That sounds so not you."

"Oh, it's very me at the moment. Anyway, you concentrate on getting a date with Lewis and don't worry about my sex life. Believe it or not, despite my own misgivings, it's come back with a bang."

Hank giggled. "Pun intended?"

"Very intended."

Chapter Five

So the drive up to Sherman Oaks for my dad's birthday celebration was, like always, a total pain. Why so many cars with just one occupant? *Look who's talking.* But it had to be bad when even the car pool lane was jammed.

"I thought you would have come earlier," was my mother's greeting after her hug and kiss.

"Mmm..." I inhaled her sweet scent. "I would've if the freeway hadn't been a parking lot. Where's Dad?"

"Outside cleaning the barbecue."

"Didn't you say you were having the party catered?"

Mom rolled her eyes. "Yes, but he insists some people might want barbecued ribs and he wants to be prepared."

"Sounds like Dad." I studied my mom for a few seconds, looking for any signs of what exactly, I wasn't sure. Aging, tiredness? "You look lovely, but you always do," I said. "Dad's not wearing you out now he's retired?"

"Not at all. His golf and his gardening keep him busy. He's hardly under my feet most of the time."

They walked out into the backyard where his father was busy scrubbing the barbecue grill tray. "Hi, Dad. Happy birthday."

"Hi, son." Ben Harrison, my dad, despite his emphysema, was still fit looking at sixty-six. Something I hoped I'd be at his age. I stepped into his hug, prolonging it just because I loved feeling the strength of his arms around me. I might have been unlucky in love of the carnal kind, but never have I ever had to doubt that my parents loved me unconditionally.

"How've you been?" he asked when I let him go.

"Good. Working hard and finally getting out and about a bit."

"No word from that bastard, I suppose?"

"No word, Dad. Just as well, really. I don't know what I'd have to say to him now."

He nodded. "How about a beer?"

"Sounds good."

"Can you both go sit over there in the corner?" Mom gave us a no-arguing look. "The caterers will be here any minute and they'll want a clear space."

Dad winked at me and went into the kitchen to fetch the beers.

"And only one before everyone gets here, Ben," Mom added. "I don't want the pair of you addled before the party starts."

"As if," I said then hugged her again. "You know your men can hold their drink."

She cuffed me lightly on the shoulder. "How are you really, darling?"

"I'm fine, Mom, really." Long as she didn't press too hard, I could fake it. The last thing I wanted was a repeat performance of my crying jag in front of Pete. "It took a while but I'm getting back in the swing of things, socially, I mean."

The chiming of the doorbell had her stepping back from my embrace. "That'll be the caterers." She passed my dad on his way out with our beers. He handed me one then signaled at the far corner of the patio.

"We should be out of the way over there," he said, chuckling.

"Wow," I exclaimed after we'd sat down out of the way and a barrage of three young men and two women flooded the patio. "How many are coming to this shindig anyway?"

"Too many," Dad groused. "She's invited people I used to work with, friends of hers from the charity work she does, neighbors and people I've never heard of." He laughed. "If they all show up, this'll be as much fun for me as it will be for you."

"We'll just have to hang out together if things get rough," I told him. "You know how the neighbors can be."

I checked out the catering guys while Dad and I talked. Not bad, especially the tall blond with biceps straining under his white shirt when he lifted some obviously heavy boxes all by himself. The doorbell chimed again.

"I'd better get that," I said, getting off my chair. "Mom's got her hands full, by the looks of things." I passed through the living room and saw yet another catering guy setting up a bar in the dining area. I paused to turn on the stereo. This party needed music! I didn't recognize the people on the doorstep, a man a woman and a young girl, but they seemed to know me, trooping past me with cries of 'Hi, Jason — good to see you again'. *Must be neighbors.*

A couple of hours later, the party was in full swing and I had talked to dozens of people I vaguely remembered. My face was stiff from having to keep a smile on it the entire time. But the neat thing was that the party was a success and Dad really seemed to be enjoying himself, and Mom was flushed with happiness that so many had shown up to celebrate his birthday. I had to wonder if there would be anywhere near this number of friends to wish me well on my sixty-sixth.

The catering staff had done a great job of keeping the food and drink flowing. I had made friends with the bartender, of course, and he'd kept my glass brimming for the past two hours or so. I was feeling no pain, but wasn't at the obnoxiously drunk stage where I would be talked about in hushed tones for weeks to come. The doorbell chimed and I glanced at my watch. A latecomer no less.

I opened the door and tried not to gape at the good-looking guy standing there, a wrapped present in his hand.

"Hi," I said.

"Hi. You don't remember me, do you, Jason?"

"Uh…"

"Noah Jamieson…we were at Clarkson High together."

"Noah…" Wait, the only Noah I'd known was some fat, asthmatic kid I'd once saved from a bunch of bullies just before I left to go to college. *That* Noah? The guy who stepped inside was almost my height. Lush auburn hair fell to one side of his forehead, feathered eyebrows topped stunning green eyes, and his mouth…his *mouth* was full and luscious and ripe for kissing. *Holy shit. Noah Jamieson.*

"Yes," I said weakly. "I remember you…but you look kinda different."

He laughed, a deeply melodious sound completely in keeping with the ravishing image he presented. "You probably remember me as fat, pimply and wheezing my ass off."

"Uh, well, I wouldn't put it quite like that. It's good to see you again. You look great."

"Thanks, you too, but then you always did. You were the one I wanted to be like more than anyone else in the world."

"Wow, that's quite a compliment. Would you like a drink?"

"Please. A Chardonnay if you have it."

"I think we have just about everything here." The bartender smiled and poured Noah a glass of wine. I stood and surveyed the man in front of me, elegant in an expensively tailored tan suit, light blue shirt and darker blue power tie. "Did you just come from work?" I asked.

"You could say that." He smiled and tipped his glass at me. "I had an appointment with a client who's very fussy about one's dress code. I was running a little late, so I decided to come directly over here afterward." He glanced outside. "I should go wish your dad a happy birthday and say hi to your mom."

"Oh yes, of course." *Wait, he's kept in touch with my parents all this time and they've never mentioned it? Yet they know him well enough to invite him to the party?* I followed him out onto the patio where he headed for a group that included both my parents.

"Noah!" My mother beamed at him and gave him a hug. "Don't you look handsome! So glad you could make it. Jason, you remember Noah, don't you?"

I nodded. *Not as well as you do.* I watched him shake hands with my father who of course pulled him in for a hug. They chatted for a few minutes then some other people came over to say hello to Noah. I felt like an outsider. What had I missed here? Shrugging, I turned away and went back to my friendly bartender who had refilled my glass. I took it but only had the tiniest sip. I had to slow down, I told myself, if I wanted to have any chance of getting to know Noah better.

He came back into the living room a few minutes later and perched on one of the barstools beside me. "So, tell me where you've been and what you've been doing for the last twelve years."

"My mom and dad haven't kept you up-to-date?"

"They said you were living in San Diego," he said, ignoring my attempted jab. "And that you'd suffered a bad breakup. I was sorry to hear that, although I considered your ex an utter fool."

I snorted. "I was the fool, Noah, for believing him."

"You were not a fool, Jason. It's easy to believe the one you're in love with."

"Speaking from experience?"

He nodded. "And I hope that, like me, you have learned from that experience."

"I'm getting there. It still hurts when I dwell on it too much, but I keep thinking that with each day that passes, I can deal a bit better."

"How long are you here for?"

"I leave Monday morning."

"Would you perhaps like to have dinner with me tomorrow night?"

I stared at his smoothly sculpted features, at the tiny smile that lifted the corner of his full lips, and I couldn't think of anything I'd like more than to spend time in his company. I tried to see the young Noah in his features, but it was almost impossible. Everything about him had been refined from pudgy adolescence to elegant adulthood.

"I would like that very much," I said sincerely.

"Good." He touched my hand with his. "You know, I have never forgotten how you stepped in and saved my ass from a beating at the hands of those bullies years ago. You were my hero for a long time afterward. Now when I look at you again, after all these years, I think you still are."

I flushed and squirmed a little on my stool. "It was nothing. You were so small…"

"And fat, and hopeless, and yet you sent those creeps on their way without so much as raising your voice. I can still see that fortitude in you, Jason. I love your name too. It fits the hero image I have of you, like Jason and the Argonauts, the guy in Greek mythology who went in search of the Golden Fleece."

Wow. I've always been amazed at how one can be seen through the eyes of another, even though this sounded a bit over the top. "Thanks," I mumbled, unable to say much more.

"Your mom said you work for a software company."

"Yeah, Sonar Electronics."

"You like it there?"

"It's okay. How about you?"

"I'm self-employed. I own a small customer service company."

He handed me a business card which read, *Noah Jamieson, B.A. Your satisfaction guaranteed.* "Oh good," I said, "now I have your phone number."

"Just don't use it to cancel dinner tomorrow."

"I wouldn't dream of it."

We exchanged smiles then he stood up. "I have to go, unfortunately, but I should say goodnight to your folks. Shall I pick you up at seven, here?"

"That'll be great."

I walked with him onto the patio and after he'd said his goodbyes went with him to the door. We stepped outside and he leaned in and kissed me on the cheek. "Goodnight, Jason. It was wonderful seeing you again."

"Goodnight. See you tomorrow." He turned and walked down the driveway to his car. *Well...* I touched my cheek where he'd kissed me. *That was an unexpected pleasure.*

The caterers cleaned up so well Mom and I had very little to do after they left. Dad said he was exhausted from all that social activity and went to bed.

"So, what did you think of Noah?" Mom asked when we'd settled on the living room couch with cups of the hot tea she had brewed.

"I was surprised. The little fat kid I remembered from school is quite the looker. He asked me to have dinner with him tomorrow night. Hope that's all right."

Mom nodded. "I think your dad will be looking for a quiet evening. We can have brunch together at Jennifer's Kitchen, if you like, around noon. Noah looks as if he's very successful, don't you think?"

"Very. So how come you know him well enough to ask him to Dad's party?"

"His mother used to drag him along to our charity events and he was so helpful once he got over his initial shyness." She smiled, remembering. "Such a sweet boy and it was lovely seeing him blossom through the years. I was so afraid for him when his mother died, but an aunt took him in until he went to college."

"I can't believe you never mentioned him to me…that he was part of your group, I mean."

"I think I might have, but you were always so caught up in your life with Darren, it probably didn't register."

"God, was I that oblivious to everything and everyone else around me?" I shuddered. "Sometimes when I look back on that time, it was like everything revolved around him. I loved him so much, Mom, I guess I didn't see how selfish I'd become. If it didn't include Darren, I wasn't interested."

"And he wasn't very interested in what mattered to you." She took my hand. "Your dad and I worried about you so many times when you'd find some excuse for you and Darren not to visit. I didn't blame you. I knew how persuasive he could be and how willing you were to please him."

"Oh shit, you make me sound like a…like a *wimp*, and a terrible son!"

She squeezed my hand. "You were never a terrible son, Jason. You just made some bad choices. Whatever, you are free now, free to make new choices. And remember that whatever they are, your dad and I will always love you."

I blinked back to tears forming in my eyes. "Well, I know for a fact I have something Darren never had."

"What's that, dear?"

I managed to grit out despite the sob that was welling in my throat, "You and Dad, the best parents in the world."

Chapter Six

Noah called promptly at seven and it was impossible not to admire the delicious sight he presented when I opened the door. This time the suit was gone, but his elegance remained, the black shirt and dark gray slacks he wore only adding to the slight air of mystery he invoked. I so wanted to know more about him.

"Come on in," I said, reaching for his hand. He took mine but didn't shake it, more like caressed it. I had a very good feeling about this evening.

Mom and Dad came over to say hello and we stood for a few minutes chatting about this and that until Noah glanced at his watch. "I made reservations for seven-thirty, so we should be on our way. Lovely seeing you both again."

I couldn't help but notice the beaming smiles both my parents wore as we left. Were they hoping for some kind of spark between Noah and me? A way for me to forget all about Darren and find someone else to fill my life?

"How was your day?" Noah asked, touching my arm.

"Good. Yours?"

"I had a lunchtime appointment then I worked out for a couple of hours or so. Nothing too exciting." He opened the passenger side door to his white Mercedes for me, waited till I'd slipped inside then closed the door gently. This was a man with manners in addition to his stunning good looks. I didn't need another man to hold doors open for me, but it was a nice touch. He slid into the driver's seat and stared at me for a moment.

"You have beautiful eyes, Jason."

"Thank you." *Please don't say bewitching.* "Yours are different, kind of exotic. I've always envied guys with green eyes."

He chuckled while he started the engine. "My ex used to say I had eyes like a cat's. Whether a compliment or not, I was never quite sure."

"What is it with exes?" I laughed weakly. "They build you up to knock you down."

"Until you don't allow that to happen anymore," Noah said, his voice flat. He added, his tone lighter, "I thought we'd go to Luigi's on Shelton Avenue. You like Italian?"

"I like Italian and Italians," I replied.

"Have you been to Italy?"

"Yes, a couple of years back. We rented a car and saw Rome, Florence, the Amalfi coast. It's a beautiful memory." I sank back into that memory of a truly fantastic two weeks in my life. Darren and I alone together, so in love, so connected. I thought we'd go on and on forever. Never for a moment thinking he'd fall out of love with me, leave me. Before I could stop it, a strangled gasp escaped my throat. "Oh shit, sorry…don't know where that came from."

He slid a hand over mine and squeezed gently. "Strange how even fond memories can bring back sorrow."

I turned to look at him. His perfect aquiline profile was set in grim lines. "You too?'

"When I let them, but tonight's not the time for that crap. I asked you out to perhaps help you forget for a short time, at least, the shithead who was crass enough to leave without an explanation."

"No need to ask where you get your information."

He smiled. "Your mom is nothing if not loyal to you, but as she put it, and I quote, 'That asshole better not ever come around here, or I'll give him a new one to play with.'"

I barked out a laugh. My mother was not known for being crude, but I had heard her on occasion let fly with the odd curse word. "Funny thing is if Darren and I ever made up, she'd accept my decision. She might not like it, but she'd never show her disdain for him, not like Darren's own parents who have never accepted his homosexuality."

"Sad."

"Yes, it is."

Our conversation stalled when he pulled into Luigi's parking lot. The maître d' gave Noah a big smile when we entered the restaurant. "Good evening, Mr. Jamieson. So good to see you again."

"Thank you, Alex. This is my friend from junior high, Jason Harrison. We have a lot to talk about so perhaps you can find us a quiet table?"

"I have just the one. This way, gentlemen, please."

Our table was set to one side of the main dining room. No door to separate us, but the sense of privacy was apparent. Noah must come here often enough to expect this kind of treatment. Good for him.

"Do you like wine, Jason?" he asked.

"I'd prefer a Scotch rocks, actually."

He nodded and ordered a Scotch for me and a glass of Chianti for himself. When our drinks were delivered, he said as we toasted each other, "I hope I can persuade you to come up more often than you have in the past. I'd hate to lose touch again after we've reconnected."

"I can certainly do that. I only have the weekends free unfortunately, and maybe you could come to San Diego when you have time."

"I'll make time, Jason." Our eyes met and he smiled. His face was beautiful when still, but the smile transformed him. There was something almost ethereal about him which added to the mystery. Like he was holding a part of himself back, although he'd been very forthcoming with his thoughts about both our exes.

The meal was delicious, the soft soothing Italianate music a wonderful backdrop to our conversation which went in and out of the past and the present…a little catching up, and some talk of the future, both a little vague on that score. When the bill came, he gave his credit card to the waiter without even glancing at the charges.

"Wait, let me split that with you," I protested.

"Next time, Jason. Tonight is my treat to celebrate our finding each other again."

"Well, thank you. Now I have to come back, if only to take you to dinner."

When we were back in his car, he asked, "Can I offer you a nightcap at my place?"

It was still fairly early, so I accepted. "If it's not too far out of your way."

"It's not. A couple of miles from your parents' house."

It was a good-looking condo building in what appeared to be a new development. His unit was spacious, a large living room and a state-of-the-art kitchen, all gleaming appliances and white tile lay off the entryway while a short hall led to another room I guessed was his bedroom, the inside of which I hoped I'd get to see.

"Scotch rocks, Jason?"

"Please." I stood at the bar that divided the living room from the kitchen. "You have a nice place."

"Thanks. I bought it after only seeing the blueprints so I could close before the prices skyrocketed."

"Good to know your business is such a success."

He smiled, and there was that mystery again. "My mother left me an inheritance which greatly helped, but the business does help with the mortgage."

"So, what is it exactly that you do?"

"Have a big sip of your drink and I'll tell you."

"It's not illegal, is it?"

"Depends on how you look at it."

"Huh?" I instinctively took a more than big sip of my drink.

He came around to where I stood, took the glass from my hand and set it on the bar, then he drew me into his arms and kissed me on my mouth. Gently at first then as I opened to him, half in surprise I have to admit, a lot more firmly. His tongue in my mouth sent a thrill down my spine straight to my balls. He tasted like I knew he would, delicious, like fine wine, while the subtle scent of his cologne filled my senses. I almost whimpered when he pulled back.

"Wow, that was...incredible, Noah. Forget about telling me what you do."

"This *is* what I do, Jason."

"I don't follow." I reached for my drink and took another long swallow.

"An hour spent with me sharing kisses and some intimate touching is a three-hundred-dollar charge."

"What?" I stared at him, my mouth open. He smiled and put a finger under my chin closing my mouth for me. "Wait, you... You're a...a..."

"A male escort is the polite term, sex worker another. Are you shocked, Jason?"

"Shocked...no, no, not shocked. Surprised maybe. You look so elegant, so, so...jeez, what's the word I'm looking for?"

"Normal?"

I stared at him again, drinking in his whole persona, his beauty, his serene expression, and for the love of me, I couldn't see him sprawled under or over some old, out-of-shape creep. *Because that's the only type of person who pays for it, right?*

"What are you thinking, Jason?"

"It... It's just that I can't imagine you, or rather I don't *want* to imagine you being pawed over by somebody who can't get it without paying for it. How do you stand it?"

"It's not a question of 'standing it', Jason." He went over to the fridge took out a bottle of wine and poured himself a glass. All of that was done with such incredible, fluid grace that once again I had to steel myself against the visions of him in the arms of some fat, dirty old man. I drained my glass.

"Can I have another?" I asked.

"Of course, but I don't want my confession being the catalyst that drives you to drink." He smiled and poured me another shot. "Let's go sit on the couch."

I followed him over to the comfy-looking sofa and plonked myself down then looked at him expectantly.

"You asked me how I could stand it," he said, leaning back into the soft pillows behind him. "When I was young, I was overweight and unattractive and no one wanted to be friends with a fat, ugly kid. I had asthma so I couldn't get into sports of any kind that involved running. I tried and almost ended up dead of an asthma attack that forced the coach to call for an ambulance. It was shortly after that episode that you caught those guys pushing me around taunting me about being a wuss and useless at everything." He paused for a moment and smiled at me. "My hero."

I wanted to put my arms around him at that moment, tell him he didn't have to do what he was doing. With his looks and poise he could do anything he wanted. Then again, Noah came across as someone who wouldn't do anything he didn't want to.

"The family doctor suggested I take up swimming," he continued, "and that somehow helped me. I guess the breathing exercises had something to do with it. It also helped me lose weight. So I stuck at it and actually won a couple of trophies at the school swim meets. You had gone on to college by that time, so you didn't get to see me discard my ugly duckling status."

"I'd love to have been there to see you win."

"Yes, that's what it's all about, isn't it? When I was the fat, ugly kid no one wanted to know me, but when I dropped the pounds and the acne cleared up and I had actually proven myself, all of a sudden I was mister popularity."

"Oh, I didn't mean it that way, Noah…"

"No, I know you didn't. After all you were the one who protected me. I hoped you had looked past the pudgy, wheezy kid and just saw someone being victimized and you had to help. I remember looking up at you and thinking you were so beautiful and kind, and I longed for the day when maybe I could be like you."

I touched his hand. "But what you do now, isn't that kinda beneath you? I don't mean to sound judgmental, but I just can't get my head around what you might have to put up with."

He took my hand in his. "Jason, if I found what I do heinous or 'beneath me' as you put it, I wouldn't do it. Believe me, there have been one or two incidences that I prefer to forget, but for the most part what I'm doing is to bring some happiness to guys that can't find it elsewhere. Men in marriages who want a walk on the wild side, young guys who are afraid to make that first move, closeted individuals who from constraints because of their careers or who might face scandal if their true nature should become known. They come to me knowing they will be safe, and for an hour or perhaps more, can find a certain satisfaction in being what they want to be."

"You make it sound like it's therapy or something."

"It is therapy, in a way. A release from stress, a fulfillment that perhaps they thought they could never have."

"How many fall in love with you?"

He laughed lightly. "Probably one or two, but most are in some form of relationship. And not all my clients want sex, just a companion for a night on the town, at the theater, at a special function they don't want to attend alone. Like yesterday when I saw you and you asked if I'd just come from work because I was wearing a suit and tie. I had accompanied a gentleman to an art exhibition and he told me the dress code required."

He raised my hand to his lips and kissed it gently. "Do you think less of me now you know what I do?"

"God, no. I think I'm a little in awe of you, and I'm sorry if you think I'm demeaning you in any way."

Still holding my hand, he pulled me closer and kissed me, on the lips this time. I opened to him immediately and his tongue, filling my mouth was like an electric jolt. He wrapped his arms around me and we fell back on the couch, with me on top of him. I fumbled with his shirt buttons and pulled the material back enough so that I could attack his left nipple. His body shuddered under me when I teased the small hard nub with my tongue and teeth.

The hardness of his cock pressed against mine and I mumbled, "Can we get naked? I want to feel all of you."

He pushed at me gently and I sat up. He stood and took my hand before leading me into the bedroom. The décor appreciation would have to wait. My hands were shaking when I undressed him as quickly as I could. I'd never felt so pent-up with desire and excitement. Not with Matt or Joey, or anyone since Darren, and I sure as hell didn't want to think about him at that moment.

Sculptors would duel to the death to get a shot at having Noah model for them. His body was, to use an old cliché, poetry in motion. Under his smooth, lightly tan skin, his muscles were clearly defined. His chest, his abdomen, all of him perfection. No wonder he could charge anything he wanted for an hour with him. All I wanted at that moment was to hold him, kiss him, hopefully give him the same kind of thrills and chills he gave me, and I found myself thinking, *Yes, I'd gladly pay for this!*

He put his hands on my shoulders and pulled me in for a long, long kiss. I went weak at the knees when he wrapped his arms around me again, holding our naked bodies pressed tightly together. My cock pulsed against his and he writhed sensuously, arching his body into mine then, with a sudden change of action, dropped to his knees and took the head of my erection between his lips. He teased for a moment or two, using the tip of his tongue to play with the slit, licking up the pre-cum.

"I knew you'd taste good," he said, smiling up at me. He slid his lips slowly down the length, paused, pulled back then dove back down again, faster, all the way to the hilt. For a moment I thought I was going to come right there and then, and wouldn't that have been embarrassing?

He ringed the base of my erection with his fingers, staying the explosion I'd been sure was about to happen. He looked up at me with those beautiful green eyes, pulled back and smiled.

"Tease," I whispered. That was all I had in me. He chuckled softly and pushed me onto the bed, following me as I sprawled backward. He straddled me then bent down to kiss my lips, my chin, my throat, and he sucked on the pulse beneath my Adam's apple, all guaranteed to drive me wild.

"Better?"

"Everything you do is better...the best." *So do something to let him know you're not just gonna lie there and let him do all the work.* I sat up and rolled him onto his back and went down on him. His cock, like him, was a thing of beauty. I mean, what else could it be, attached to him? I could've searched every centimeter of his body and found nothing but perfection. If those fools that had taunted and bullied him in school could see him now, they would have to bow in awe of him. Okay, maybe I was getting a little carried away, but he really was amazing. And his cock…so hot and hard, long with an upward curve toward his navel. I gripped it at the base and sucked the pre-cum from the slit, letting it pool on my tongue so I could savor the tangy taste. *Delicious…*

I sank my lips down the hot length and scraped gently at the base with my teeth. His body bucked at the sensation and he moaned from deep in his throat. Sexy as hell. I sucked long and hard. He ran his fingers through my hair and arched into my mouth.

"*Jason…*" His voice was thick and he started to pull away. *Oh, no you don't…* He was on the edge and I wanted to taste all he had to give. I pushed my hands under his butt and cupped the twin round globes, pulling him up as I sucked harder. He thrashed under me and he came with an excited shout, his semen flooding my mouth with such force that I had difficulty swallowing it all. But I did, and continued to hold him there so I could lick every last vestige from him.

After a few moments he said, "I think I'd like you to fuck me."

I was all up for that and told him so. He reached for his nightstand drawer and brought out a condom and lube. He ripped off the foil wrapper then put the condom between his lips and sent a thrill down my spine when he slipped the condom over my throbbing erection using only his mouth. He winked at me then lay back, pulling me toward him then winding his legs around my waist. I grabbed the lube bottle as he raised his hips, giving me clear access. I lubed up my fingertips and inserted one then two fingers inside him.

He gasped as I touched his prostate then went deeper. He moaned and gazed up at me through narrowed eyes. He raised his legs higher and I set the lube aside and guided myself toward his entrance. His heat was intense and for a terrible moment I thought I might spill inside the condom before I was completely inside him. He wrapped his legs around my waist and lifted his hips. A groan of rapture escaped me as I slid all the way in. I'm not huge, but big enough to give pleasure and Noah's face reflected that as I moved inside him, making sure I gave his sweet spot the attention I was sure he craved.

"Feels so good, Jason," he murmured, stroking my face, running his thumb over my lower lip. I sucked it into my mouth and he bucked under me, driving himself onto my erection. "Go faster," he said. "I won't break." And truth to tell I was being careful of not hurting him. His words inspired me to ram harder into him and he grinned up at me. "That's it, Jason, give it to me, fuck me!"

And I did, ramming into him like I was possessed, and he clung to me, arms and legs wrapped around me, rising to kiss me on the lips, suck and bite my neck and shoulders and send me spinning off into the greatest orgasm of my life. I roared when I came, plunging harder and deeper into him and he cried out as he pumped his cock to completion, his hot creamy cum spraying all over his abs and chest. Dizzy as I was from my climax, I couldn't resist running my tongue into the still warm puddle of semen in his navel and trailing it up over his torso to his waiting lips. We sucked on each other's tongues, I relishing the saltiness of his cum I shared with him.

"Don't worry about bite marks on your neck," he said after we'd lain quietly together for few minutes, he nuzzling the area he'd sucked on earlier. "I know how not to leave hickeys."

I wouldn't have minded although I probably would have to explain them to my fellow workers' and friends' inquisitive stares.

"You will stay the night with me?" he asked, brushing his lips over mine.

"Just try getting rid of me," I kidded him.

We got up to shower together and there was another memory I thought I might treasure forever. The sight and feel of his smooth, athletic body shimmering with water and soapy bubbles was a vision I knew I could jerk off to, until we met again.

Chapter Seven

Being back at work seemed almost surreal. I didn't want to be there. It was like I didn't belong anymore. Thoughts of Noah hadn't left my head since we'd said goodbye Monday morning. I hadn't wanted to leave but he had an eleven o'clock appointment, and I did have to go home and tell my parents goodbye – but just the sound of the word 'appointment' made me feel sick to my stomach, now that I knew what it meant.

The hours spent with him had been sensational. Yes, I told myself, this is what he did, made the one he was with feel special, loved, wanted, needed. All the feelings he had instilled in me. And that was what I had to keep reminding myself. Noah was a professional. He gave pleasure for a price. I hated to think about the kind of bill I'd racked up. I had carefully avoided mentioning it. Even to kid about it might have sounded crass.

"Have a good long weekend?" Hank asked when I met him at the coffee machine.

"Yeah, it was great. I hadn't realized how much I needed a change of scenery, even if it was just at my mom and dad's house. The party was a big success, and I met someone."

"You did?" Hank's eyes widened. "At your parents' house?"

"Yeah, believe it or not. He was at Clarkson High, same as me, but I didn't really get to know him well then. I was leaving to go to college. But he remembered me and we had fun catching up."

"And?"

"And what?"

"And what else?" Hank rolled his eyes. "Don't expect me to believe nothing happened between you."

"Uh, yeah…we got together, but he's a really busy guy…so no expectations."

"Oh, that's too bad."

"How about you and Lewis?" I asked, mostly trying for a quick change of subject, but at the same time, I did hope they'd seen each other again after that night in the bar.

"Oh, he's amazing!" Hank reddened and looked warily around to see if anyone had heard his outburst. I laughed and that made him blush more.

"That good, huh?"

"Yeah, that good. But it's not just that. I've never met a guy before who actually seems to *like* me. We spend hours just talking and he's a really interesting guy and—"

We had to cut it short when John and Phil approached the coffee area. Neither man looked at us, but there were no snide comments thrown our way, so maybe they'd learned their lesson. Still, I didn't like the atmosphere they created with their stupidity and I knew that at some point I was going to tell them just that.

William called us both into his office at that point. "I have another project for you two since you did so well together on that last one," he told us. "And again, it's a rush job. Don't know why these guys can't get their act together. They leave everything to the last minute."

"That's okay," I said. "We like the challenge, don't we, Hank?" Hank nodded, but I was thinking this was just what I needed to take my mind off Noah. After all, I had some crazy memories to tide me over until we could get together again.

* * * *

After work I decided to go home and take it easy for a change. Bobby's Tavern might hold unknown goodies, but after the hours spent with Noah, I figured no one else was going to satisfy me the way he could. I might call Pete later in the week just to keep in touch like he'd asked me to. Once back at my place, I changed into shorts and a T-shirt, threw a frozen macaroni cheese into the microwave and got myself a beer from the fridge.

Lying on the couch, I fiddled with the remote trying to find a movie on Netflix. The *ping* of the microwave coincided with the chime of my cell phone. *Wouldn't you know it?* I was hungry so the call could wait but then I glanced at the screen and saw Noah's name there. The TV dinner could wait!

"Hey," I gushed. "How are you?"

"Hi, Jason. I'm good."

Oh, that's the understatement of the year…

"You've been on my mind since you left," he said. That made me feel warm all over. "I was wondering if you would do me a favor."

Anything. "Of course."

"I have a client who is going to be in San Diego this weekend for a business meeting. He wanted me to be his dinner companion, but I have a prior engagement. So I wondered if you would fill in for me? This is totally legit, Jason. No sex will be involved, just dinner and conversation, perhaps drinks afterward, depending on how late dinner is. Your fee will be three hundred dollars per hour and, of course, dinner. He has a favorite restaurant there and he will make the reservations. What d'you think?"

"Wow…I-I don't know." Truth was I was disappointed that this was the reason he'd called. Not to just talk or plan our next get together. "Uh…what if I'm not up to his standard of dinner companions? It could be awkward, couldn't it?"

Noah chuckled. "Simon is a very nice man, very sociable, so there won't be any awkwardness. I've already told him I can't make it but I would try to find him a suitable replacement. I know he'll like you, Jason. This would be of great help to me if you'd agree."

Well, I certainly didn't want to let him down, so… "If you're sure he'll be okay with me as a substitute."

"Jason, you'll be more than a mere substitute. You are a very attractive man. He'll be delighted. I presume you have a suit and tie? It'll be kind of formal."

"Yeah, I have a couple of suits for conventions and stuff."

"Great. Okay, his name is Simon Foster and he'll be staying at the Hyatt. I'll send a photograph of him to your phone and I'll give him your number. He'll call you when he gets to town and give you his schedule. The only definite date is dinner on Friday night. If he asks you to join him again, it will be the usual fee of three hundred dollars per hour. Okay?"

"O-okay. I was hoping we'd have a chance to see each other again soon."

"I'm hoping for that too, Jason. I have a pretty hectic schedule for the next couple of weeks, but maybe after that we can fix something up."

"Sounds good." It didn't sound good, but I wasn't about to start whining and seen as needy this early on in our friendship.

"Sounds *very* good, and thanks so much for doing this for me. I'll be in touch in the week just to firm things up. Bye for now."

"Bye." I ended the call and sat for a few minutes thinking over what Noah had asked me to do. He had it made it seem like no big deal. Meet a guy, have dinner with him, pick up three hundred dollars. The no-sex part of it was okay. As much sex as I'd had in the past week or so I still couldn't do it with just anyone. I had my standards after all, I told myself, laughing quietly. My cell chimed and there was the photo of Simon Foster that Noah had said he'd send me. He was a nice-looking older man with silver hair and a friendly smile. Nothing scary there, and one if I'd met at a convention or business meeting, I might have shared a conversation with.

So this was going to be okay. Maybe I wouldn't charge him the three hundred, just tell him dinner was enough. Or would that put Noah in a bad light? Was there some kind of male-escort code about not attempting to undercut the competition? *What am I talking about?* Noah wasn't competition, and it was laughable that he would even think of me in that way.

Besides, I might never hear from this Simon guy and that would be okay too.

I remembered my TV dinner, which was now probably a congealed mess. It was, so I threw it in the trash and made myself a tuna sandwich instead.

* * * *

Hank and I were busy with our project for the next three days. William gave us one of the meeting rooms with a large table so we could spread out our blueprints. I had to admit Hank was easy to work with. We enjoyed a few laughs and he told me more about Lewis, who sounded like a good guy from Hank's description, but I had to decline an invitation to join them for a drink on Friday night.

"Sorry, I'm meeting a friend on Friday," I told him. He looked disappointed, but I figured once he was in Lewis's company, I wouldn't be missed. Simon Foster had left a message on my phone saying he was looking forward to meeting me and he'd be at the Belvidere downtown at seven on Friday if I'd like to join him for a cocktail before dinner. *Wow, classy place.* I'd better wear my best bib and tucker for this night out.

Matt called me on Wednesday night hoping to see me on Thursday. I said yes and he was ever the eager lover. Of course, being a jerk, I had to compare his lovemaking with Noah's and he came up short. Not 'down there'. He could never be called short in that department, but the thrill just wasn't there. Afterward, I blamed myself. I'm not arrogant enough to rule out the fact it could've been my fault that our union wasn't brilliant like the time before. Maybe my actions hadn't been as ardent as on our first couple of times together.

Had Noah spoiled me for everyone else just like Darren had? I sure hoped not 'cause I had a feeling I wouldn't be seeing him nearly enough in the next few weeks.

* * * *

Simon Foster was, as Noah had told me, a really nice guy. Older, confident, with impeccable manners and a quiet sense of humor, he was a delight to be around. I think we covered every topic we possibly could. It was good we agreed on most things, even on politics, so there were no awkward pauses during our conversations. After dinner I drove him back to his hotel. He didn't ask me up to his room and I was unsure how I felt about that. Relieved in a way, but I wondered if it reflected poorly on my social skills. Noah had said there would be no sex, and I guessed, rightly as I later found out, that Simon adhered always to their arrangement.

Before he left me, he stuck something in my top pocket and asked if he could call me tomorrow. I said, "Of course," and when I got home, I found he had paid me an extra hundred dollars. Okay, so he must have enjoyed himself. Good to know. I wondered if I should call Noah and tell him how it went. I decided to let him call me, and went to bed.

Simon called me mid-afternoon and invited me to a small gathering at a client's house in La Jolla. I said yes, and arranged to pick him up at his hotel and drive him to the party. The house was amazing, even by La Jolla standards, situated in a gated community high in the hills and with a really beautiful view of the ocean. The hosts, a husband and wife of indeterminate age — they'd both had some advanced plastic surgery — were charming, and insisted I call them by their first names…Lois and Charlie. "No stuffiness here," Charlie exclaimed, shepherding us into an enormous living room where several other people were gathered.

Simon knew some of them and introduced me as his San Diego friend. I was pretty sure they were aware what that meant, but were friendly and gracious. I didn't feel totally awkward, but I made for the bar after asking Simon what he'd like to drink. There was a guy standing there talking to the bartender, and oh boy, was he hot! Tall and tan and blond and handsome, he would have been a standout on any runway or at any high-end gathering.

He turned to me, smiled and introduced himself. "Hi, I'm Bruce."

"Jason," I said in reply and shook the hand he proffered. I ordered Simon's and my drinks. He followed me over to where Simon stood chatting with his friends and stayed at my side while I handed Simon his drink. It seemed that Simon already knew Bruce, as they exchanged polite nods.

"Is Janis here tonight?" Simon asked him.

"Over there." Bruce pointed vaguely at another group at the far end of the room.

"Ah yes." Simon looked across the room and I followed his gaze till it rested on an older woman, who wore an elegant black and white long dress.

Okay, so Bruce was either her son, which I doubted, or he was fulfilling the same role as me. I guess *Janis* saw us looking for she smiled and waved then walked slowly toward us. She rested her hand on Bruce's arm and he bent slightly to kiss her cheek.

"Simon, I haven't seen you in ages, and who is this delightful young man with you?"

I was introduced then she and Simon fell into conversation. Bruce touched my arm and led me off to the side. "So, you're Simon's boytoy?"

It struck me as funny rather than crass. One boytoy to another? "Dinner companion," I told him, after a sip of the very good Scotch I'd been served. "I'm actually doing this as a favor for a friend. He couldn't make it. I've never done this before, but Simon's very nice and, so far, has kept his hands to himself."

Bruce grinned. "You should do it more often. You've got the looks, and if I'm not mistaken…" He put a finger inside my jacket and ran it over my chest. "You've got the bod too."

I looked over at Simon's group to make sure no one was watching us, but they were all deep in conversations. "They seem like a nice bunch of people."

"They're a bunch of letches. Don't let the sophisticated veneer fool you."

"You have a boyfriend?" I asked.

"Why, are you applying for the position?"

I laughed. "No."

"What makes you think I'm gay anyway?"

I shrugged. "Takes one to know one, so they say."

"I'm bisexual. Makes it easier when I have to lay someone like Janis over there. After a while, there's not much difference. I learned a long time ago to shut out desire and just get the job done."

"Ouch. That's a bit soulless, isn't it?"

He downed the last of his drink and stared at me for a long moment. "Getcha another?" he asked, glancing at my glass.

"No thanks. I think I'll join the man who's paying for my time."

"Suit yourself," he said and hurried toward the bar.

Well, that was interesting, but for sure I'm not applying to be his *boyfriend.*

"Did you have a good time, Jason?" Simon asked a few hours later as we sped along the I-5 toward the Hyatt. I thought it was sweet of him to care whether I'd enjoyed myself or not.

"Yes, it was very nice, Simon."

"I saw you in conversation with Janis Landon's young man."

"Yeah, he's a character."

"He's very lucky to have Janis as his sponsor. She's included him in her will, and she is worth a fortune."

"Lucky indeed," I said.

"That's what you young men should do, you know. Find a very wealthy patron, treat them well and reap the benefits of their wealth."

I glanced at him in surprise. "That's all right with you? That you'd let someone like Bruce, in a way, con you?" It pained me to think of a nice guy like Simon being taken advantage of. Was that what Noah was doing?

"Not me," Simon said firmly. "For a start, I'm not *that* wealthy. I have enough to ensure that my family's taken care of and my grandchildren will go to college if they wish, with no student debt."

"Oh, you're married?"

"I was. My wife died ten years ago…cancer."

"I'm sorry. So, this thing with Noah…and me…?"

"I like the company of young men, Jason. It makes me feel alive. I don't ask for sex. Quite honestly, the idea of having someone as beautiful as Noah, or yourself, having to pleasure an old man like me, I find quite sickening."

"But you're still a handsome man, Simon. I don't think anyone would find having sex with you a chore."

"Would you have sex with me, Jason?" I guess I hesitated too long because he said, "I didn't think so, but no hard feelings."

"Wait, I didn't say anything. I think the next thing I say should be, would you have sex with me?"

He laughed lightly. "I'd be a fool to refuse you, but I will. Not because you're not attractive, but because for several years I have been impotent, and it's no fun for me anymore. So, I thank you for being so nice and making an old man feel alive again, if only for a few hours. May I call you when I'm in San Diego again in a month's time?"

"If it's okay with Noah. I don't want to step on his toes. This is his profession, after all."

"That is very good of you. Don't worry, I'll take care of Noah. Ah, here we are."

I pulled up in front of the hotel and leaned over to kiss his cheek. "Thanks, Simon. It has been a pleasure being with you."

He shoved some pre-folded money into my pocket then took out his wallet and peeled off another two one-hundred-dollar bills.

"No, Simon, that's not necessary."

"It is very necessary. You have been a wonderful companion."

"What time does your plane leave tomorrow?"

"Nine a.m. I believe."

"I'll pick you up and take you, if you like."

"That's not necessary. A few of us are going in a company limo, but again I thank you, Jason. You are a delight."

I watched until he was safely inside the hotel entry then I pulled slowly away. In two nights, I had made almost a thousand dollars. My savings account would gasp when I deposited the cash on Monday. All I'd done was keep a nice man company. Who knew this kind of thing was possible? For some reason I'd always pitied guys who gave it up for money, but here was a whole different slant to the idea of male escorts. Then I remembered what Bruce had said at the party. It was obvious he slept with Janis Landon and what he'd said — *'I learned a long time ago to shut out desire and just get the job done'* — made me shudder.

No way in hell could I have sex with anyone I didn't desire, even if only for as long as it took to get each other off. There had to be some kind of connection, some warmth, some *feeling* — or so I thought.

Chapter Eight

Noah called me late Sunday night. He sounded tired but said he wanted to thank me for treating Simon so well.

"He's a sweet, generous guy," I said. "Uh…did he say anything about seeing me again?"

"No, did he ask you?"

"He said he'd be back here in a month and could he call me? I told him I didn't want to be stepping on your toes."

"You wouldn't be."

"He did say he'd take care of you, regardless."

Noah chuckled. "Yeah, he's good that way. Well, if you want to see him again, it's okay with me."

"You're sure?"

"Totally. As a matter of fact…" He paused as if thinking. "Um, I know I said I was busy for the next couple of weeks but there's a scene you might be interested in next Saturday."

"A scene?"

"Yeah, something that is planned ahead. This guy I know likes three-ways and I've never been comfortable with the kind of guy he brings, usually someone he's picked up in a bar the night before. If I told him I could bring someone he'd really like, would you be interested in going with me? There'll be a fee for you, of course."

A three-way. I'd never been involved in one. Darren had always been enough for me, and I'd put Noah in that category, too. But he'd be there and if I concentrated on him, maybe I'd enjoy it. But that wasn't the point, was it? It was the client who had to enjoy it. If he wanted to kiss me, maybe even fuck me, I'd have to fake the enjoyment part, and I didn't know how good I'd be at that.

"I-I don't know, Noah. You might think I'm a bit naïve, but I've never done that, and with someone I don't even know, I'm not sure I could."

"You'll like Russ. He's a sweet guy. This is his only kink so it's not like he'll tie you up or blindfold you. He's pretty vanilla—he just likes to have two people in bed with him."

"Okay, I'll do it if you'll be there. Maybe you can give me some pointers on what's expected of me."

"Jason, just be yourself. He'll like you, I know it."

I wasn't sure how he could know the guy would like me. I mean, I'm good-looking enough, I suppose, but I don't pretend I'm everyone's cup of java.

"Okay then, that's settled. If you come to my house at five on Saturday, I'll have a little snack ready for you before we go over to Russ's."

I couldn't pretend I wasn't excited, mostly because I'd be seeing Noah again, and if having sex with another guy was the only way of having sex with Noah,

I was up for it. *Just remember this is business,* I told myself, trying to quell my excitement. It didn't work.

* * * *

The week went by quickly enough. We were busy at work and I enjoyed listening to Hank extol Lewis's virtues when we had time together to talk, mostly at lunchtime. According to Hank, Lewis was a god come down to earth, his only purpose to make Hank the happiest man on the face of this planet. I didn't want to pop his balloon of bliss by asking him to be cautious which I was sure he would have seen as negativity, so I smiled and nodded until he said, rather snippily, "Okay, you don't believe a word of this, do you?"

"Of course, I do."

"Liar."

"Hank, I'm hurt."

He snorted. "I know you've been around a lot more than me. I think I even confessed that I didn't know diddly-squat about guys or sex, or having sex with guys, but Lewis is different from what you described. He's big, everywhere, but he's gentle and he listens to me, and I'm in love with him."

Oh, boy. As glad as I was to know that Lewis was big *everywhere*, glad for Hank that is, I was sure I could sense disaster ahead. "Have you told him you love him?"

"No."

"Don't. I mean, don't rush it," I added, seeing his eyebrows arch dangerously. "It's only been a week, Hank. Let him be the one to say it first."

He sighed. "I guess you're right, O wise one, but, Jason, I have never been with anyone like him. He's so beautiful. His eyes, his mouth, his body, his — "

"Okay, TMI, Hank. I intend on hopefully seeing Lewis now and then in the future, so I don't want to be checking him out every time he stands in front of me."

"You mean you haven't?" Hank threw me a look of disbelief. "I saw how your eyes widened when you met him in the bar that night."

"Yeah, okay, he's hot and you are one lucky guy, Hank. So, don't screw it up by pushing too hard."

Of course, I should listen to my own advice sometimes. During the next few days, I heard from both Matt and Joey, and even Kelly sent me a text saying he'd be back in town the following week, and could we get together? I ignored them all, which wasn't very nice of me, but I knew what they wanted and frankly I was not into having sex with anyone but Noah. Was I falling into the same trap I'd warned Hank about? And where was all the angst I'd gone through after losing Darren?

Was I falling in love with Noah? That would be a really bad idea, I told myself. A *really* bad idea. Noah was incredible without a doubt. Probably the most beautiful man I'd ever met, Darren included. I could do a Hank and list all his physical attributes just like Hank had listed Lewis's, and I could add Noah's sweet smile, his ability to make me feel special when were together, which when I was thinking rationally had been exactly twice. We'd had sex on only one of those occasions. Did the fact we'd had sex three times in that one night count as more?

More importantly than all that, Noah was a professional male escort. He had probably hardened his heart against falling in love with any of his clients a long time ago. How else could he do what he did? Yes, I was sure we'd had more of a connection than client-escort, but maybe that had all been one-sided — my side. He'd been in love. He had an ex, someone we never really got around to discussing. We'd been too busy with other things, much better things, but now I was curious about what had happened to end their relationship.

* * * *

Saturday traffic to Los Angeles was always pitiful and this Saturday was no exception. I was glad I'd left earlier than I usually did for the trip, but even so it was almost five-thirty when I pulled into Noah's parking lot. I had called him ahead of time to let him know I'd be late and he was his usual unruffled self. He greeted me with a big, long kiss that made me hope, maybe, just maybe he was more than just fond of me.

Out of his usual formal wear, he looked even better. He had on a black muscle shirt that did just what it was supposed to do, displaying his biceps and chest muscles to perfection.

"Would you like to shower?" he asked when he let me go. "You must be sticky from sitting in your car all this time."

"A shower sounds good. I'll be quick."

He grinned and patted my butt. "Pay attention to this. Russ likes to rim."

"Oh…okay."

After showering, and duly paying attention to the area Noah had indicated, I changed into the outfit I'd brought. Noah had said it was to be casual sporty. Russ liked his men to look like jocks, apparently. I'd brought a sleeveless gray T-shirt, black shorts and trainers, and after checking myself out in the mirror thought I looked as much like a jock as I ever would. Noah seemed to appreciate it when I exited the bathroom.

"Very nice." He gave me another kiss then guided me over to the kitchen counter where he'd laid out a cold salmon salad, and a glass of sparkling water each. "This is light enough to go to work on. I don't like to eat a heavy meal or drink before an appointment." We settled on the bar stools and he picked up his glass of wine. "Here's to our first three-way together."

There'll be more? "Our first?" I gasped.

"Well, I thought that if you don't dislike it, the next time I have a request from Russ, I would ask you to join me. I'd much rather the fee went to you than some lug picked up in a bar." He put his hand on my bare thigh and squeezed it gently. "Would that be all right?"

"Oh, yeah. Like I said, if you're there, I'm up for it."

He leaned across and kissed me, his lips lingering on mine just long enough to give me an erection. "I do like spending time with you, Jason," he murmured.

"The feeling is mutual," I murmured back, brushing our lips together. He leaned away and tackled his salad.

"We have to get cracking," he said around a mouthful of salmon. "Russ lives in Pasadena. It's not far, but there's only street parking so it can be hectic at this time of the day."

I hated to rush through such a delicious meal, the best I'd had all week, but I wasn't going to be the one to make us late for an appointment, so after we'd thrown the dishes in the dishwasher and brushed our teeth, we were on the road. Noah drove his Mercedes although he told me he hated leaving it out on the street.

"So far, I've not had any scratches or dents from passing vandals, and just hope I continue to be lucky. Russ swears the street he lives on is very safe, but you never know." He smiled that smile of his and my heart raced. "How d'you feel about this, Jason? Are you nervous?"

"I admit to some tension, really because I've never dreamed of doing this, but like I said, you're there, so I'll be okay."

He squeezed my thigh again. "Russ will love you, I know, so just relax."

When he pulled onto Russ's street, I could see what he meant. There was parking on one side only and not a space to be seen.

"We'll go around the block and see what we can find."

He seemed quite optimistic but after we'd cruised five or six streets, I could see he was getting frustrated. He glanced at his watch several times and muttered 'damn' each time. It was just seven, but we were a good ten-minute walk away from where we had to be. Finally, he said, "Screw it," and pulled into a shopping center parking lot.

"We might get lucky and not get towed if I find an out-of-the-way space." We did. There were fewer cars around, which was a good sign. "Okay, let's go." He pulled out his cell and punched in a number. "Hi, Russ, Noah. We're here but had a bitch of a time parking. Should be with you in a few." He hung up and glanced at me. "He's okay."

Russ's apartment was in an old fifties-style building that had definitely seen better days. I was surprised as I had suspected that Noah only dealt with high-end clients.

"Not what you expected?" He must have seen my *what's this?* expression.

"Frankly, no."

"It's better inside."

Russ was a robust-looking guy in his mid-forties, I guessed. Wavy brown hair topped a pleasant, smiley face. He had a broad hairy chest and torso, muscular legs, and he was hung quite nicely. I could tell all this because he was standing there, naked.

"Come on in," he said and held out his hand. "I'm Russ and you must be Jason. Noah was right—you are a beauty. Take your clothes off. We're gonna have fun tonight, boys." He shook my hand until I thought my arm might be dislocated. Russ was exuberant, I'd give him that. Either that, or he was high. After he finished trying to shake my hand off, he pulled me in for a kiss then pushed me away and wrapped his arms around Noah who I noticed had removed his shirt.

"Oh yeah," Russ crowed after he let Noah go. "Two of the hottest guys on the planet. Maybe *the* hottest guys!"

I laughed as I stripped. I mean, how should I respond to a statement like that? I was going to ask myself that several times because Russ continued his chattering throughout the two hours we were there. The only time he shut up was when his face was buried in my ass and he was rimming me so thoroughly I wanted to ask him if he'd like to move in! Noah fucked him while he rimmed me and his moans and growls only added to his already amazing technique.

After Russ came with Noah's help, he fell asleep and Noah and I took a quick shower together. I couldn't believe two whole hours had passed. *Time surely does fly when you're having fun!*

"How d'you feel?" Noah asked while soaping my back.

"Good." I turned my head so I could kiss him.

"Would you like to spend the night with me? Go home tomorrow?"

Would I? What a silly question. "I'd love to. Can I take you to breakfast before I leave?" I knew he'd have an 'appointment' at some point during the day.

"I have a two o'clock, so breakfast would be nice." He slipped his arms around me and I pressed my butt into his groin. He chuckled. "I think we better go so we can take this further at my place."

I was all for that. We dried off and dressed quickly. Russ was snoring when we re-entered his bedroom. *He really is a trusting soul,* I thought. I hoped he was more careful if he brought someone back that he didn't know. Noah picked up an envelope that was lying on the kitchen table, then he scribbled a quick note of thanks and signed it Noah and Jason. We left and Noah flipped the lock on the door so it couldn't be opened from the outside.

The walk back to the parking lot seemed to take forever, probably because I was keyed up at the thought of Noah and I getting cozy when we got back to his place. Thankfully the Mercedes was still in its spot and unvandalized. Once we settled inside, he opened the envelope and handed me four one-hundred-dollar bills.

"Thanks." I stuffed them in pocket then ran a hand over his thigh. "Can I ask you something?"

"Sure."

"You mentioned you had an ex, but you didn't say very much about him. Call me curious, but I've wondered what happened between you and him?"

He sighed. "I made the mistake of falling in love with a client. I thought we could make it work. He certainly was into making it work in the beginning. But like all things that sound or appear too good to be true, it turned out to be exactly that."

"Was this recent?"

"No, a year ago. I'd been escorting for only a few months when I met him. He was everything I wanted. Not just physically, although he was stunning to look at, but we seemed connected somehow. *Sympatico*, I think it's called. He moved in here with me, and that's when it all went to hell."

"I'm sorry," I said. "Was he abusive?"

He nodded. "Vincent's problem was he hated being gay. He wasn't out to his family and only one or two of his friends. It made living with him a nightmare and when I protested, he became a maniac, screaming and ranting and breaking stuff. A neighbor called the cops during one of his rages.

"They arrested him, mainly because he took a swing at one of the cops. He was only in jail overnight, but he blamed me for the whole thing. He punched me, gave me a shiner which meant I had to cancel several appointments. The crazy thing was he had no objections to living with a male escort, probably because I was making good money. I left and went to stay with a friend, hoping that by some miracle he'd calm down, call me and apologize. He didn't and when I went back to my condo, he had trashed the place."

"Did you call the police?"

"No. My friends said I should, but at that point I just wanted him out of my life. The last I heard was he'd moved back to London. Did I mention he was English?"

"No, but I thought the Brits' motto was 'Keep calm and carry on'."

He chuckled. "Not that Brit. Anyway, that's the story. Not the most glamorous, I'm afraid, but it taught me that mixing business with pleasure was really foolish. I've met many wonderful guys in the time I've been escorting, but I keep them all in perspective, and never let them get too close."

I had a feeling he wasn't just referring to clients by telling me this. I made a mental note to rein in the feelings I was beginning to have for him. The last thing I wanted was to lose his friendship. When we had sex, I just had to learn to keep it on that level.

Which, when he started kissing me once we were back in his place, was far from easy. He was just so darned beautiful and warm, and oh, my God, so sexy. It would the simplest thing in the world to fall madly in love with him, but I knew I could and should not. And that knowledge both strengthened and confounded me.

"I have to go," I said, after one of his long, slow kisses that came close to melting my knee-caps.

He stared at me in surprise. "Why? I thought you were going to stay the night."

"I-I can't. I have a busy day tomorrow and need an early start."

"Jason, you're not working tomorrow. It's Sunday."

"Uh, right, but I forgot, I-I promised a friend I'd meet him for brunch, or-or was it lunch?"

He stepped back from our embrace. "Jason, if you don't want to stay with me, that's fine, but please don't make up silly excuses like the one you just spluttered your way through."

My face grew hot. "Oh, dammit, Noah. You don't want to hear this, but I-I'm starting to have feelings for you...feelings that you told me earlier could be anathema to our kind of business relationship. Because that's what it is, isn't it?"

He stared at me for a long moment with an expression I found hard to read. Then he said, "That, and I am also very fond of you. I told you I considered you my hero and I haven't changed my mind about that. But here's the thing, Jason...you are still smarting from the pain of having your relationship with Darren fall apart. You're looking for someone to fall in love with, to help you get over that loss. That's perfectly understandable, but I don't want to be the one to catch you on the rebound. That's a recipe for disaster and I don't think either you or I could handle a second loss in such a short space of time."

I nodded, knowing that what he said made complete sense, but God, it still rankled and it made me feel like a bit of a fool. "You're right," I said finally. "I'm over-reaching, searching for the one to make me forget about that son-of-a-bitch. Thank you for not pitying me enough to pretend you have feelings for me."

"I do have feelings for you, Jason." He cupped my face and kissed me gently. "I said I was very fond of you, and that won't go away any time soon. But let's not make more of it than it is."

I sighed and nodded again. "I'm gonna go, but I'd like for us to stay in touch if that's okay with you?"

"Of course, it is. You can stay here if you'd rather not face driving this time of night."

For a moment, I hesitated. What the hell was wrong with me? He was still offering me his bed. Anything could and most probably would happen in there. We could have sex, I could explore that fantastic body of his, kiss those lush lips…and I would vow not to fall in love him. I could do that, couldn't I?

I sighed. "No, it's okay. Traffic should be lighter, right now."

"Okay. I'll walk you to your car."

We stood outside for a few moments before I left. I felt as if he had more to say, but the silence between us reached the awkward stage. I gave him a hasty kiss on the cheek then slid inside my car and after a quick wave drove away. I could see him still standing there when I glanced at my rearview mirror.

"Dammit!" Me and my fool mouth had really screwed it all up. I brushed away the tears forming in my eyes. When would I ever grow up?

Chapter Nine

Halfway through the week I returned one of Matt's voicemails. I honestly didn't know I'd made such an impression on him. I figured after I had ignored his calls, he'd blow me off and move on, but he'd left three messages since I got back from Los Angeles.

"Hi, Matt."

"Hey, I thought you'd skipped town or something. How are you?"

"Just fine. Wanna grab a bite to eat sometime this week?"

"I'm off tomorrow night. How about if I bring a pizza over to your place?"

I knew what that meant, pizza first then sex, or maybe the other way around. "Okay, that sounds good. I get off at six, so let's say seven-ish?"

"See you then," he said, sounding happy.

I didn't know if having him come over was a good idea, or what, but Matt was good company and good in bed, and I needed some of that. After the incident with Noah, I'd been out of sorts since I got back and Hank had noticed and wanted to pry an explanation from me. I couldn't tell him the real story so I sort of fluffed it off and he wasn't happy with me. Oh well, he had Lewis to look forward to at the weekend, so he'd get over my funky mood faster than I would.

Matt came over the following night looking like sex on a stick in a T-shirt with an open tear over the chest that showed his left nipple, and shorts that displayed his package and bubble butt, leaving nothing to the imagination. He threw the pizza box down on the kitchen counter and grabbed me in a hug that almost broke a rib and a kiss that was wet and dirty and everything I needed at that moment.

He marched me through to the bedroom, tearing at my clothes as we went and his own after he'd thrown me onto the bed. He launched himself on top of me, kissing me from head to toe and everywhere in between. He was his eager self and I returned his passion with at least as much as I was getting. He was hard to resist and my earlier bland feeling the last time we'd had sex seemed to have disappeared in a heated rush.

He wanted to fuck me and I was fine with it, but once he'd sheathed himself and lubed me up, I gazed at his handsome face and held his eyes with mine.

"Matt," I whispered. "Slow it down. I want you to fuck me long and slow. I want to feel you all the way deep inside me like we were one."

He frowned, but he nodded and entered me slowly and with great deliberation…then he smiled. "Oh yeah," he murmured. "Yeah, Jason, feels good. For you too?"

I returned his smile, touched that he would think to ask me. "Yes, lover, so good, the best."

He leaned in for a kiss and I wrapped my arms around his neck and held him there while he kissed me and my tongue probed every corner of his mouth. I breathed through my nose to prolong the thrill. Matt could kiss and no mistake, and so could Noah — and *no, not going there*. Noah could not be a part of this. This was all me and Matt and him giving me a hundred percent, and I... Well, I came when he started ramming into me like a pile driver, those muscular hips of his letting me have it and telling me he was tired of playing slow and mellow.

Sweat streamed off his face as he plowed into me and I licked it off his lips and told myself I loved the salty tanginess of him. Matt was a sex machine and he loved doing what he did so well, and I was right there enjoying his wildness to the max. Especially when while he went on fucking me, he licked my cum off my chest and kissed me over and over until I was delirious and he blasted inside me with a cry of triumph I was sure shook the walls of my apartment.

Afterward, he rolled off me, panting and sweating up a storm, and smiling like he'd won the sexual marathon of the decade. "Christ, that was *amazing*," he gasped. He propped himself on one arm and leaned over me, an expression of concern on his pretty mug. "Was it good for you, too, Jason?"

Again, touched that he bothered to ask through his own euphoria, I nodded and whispered, "You're the best." No way was he ever going to know that I had just lied to him.

* * * *

Hank was becoming no slouch in the sexual nosiness arena. He eyed me suspiciously when we met at the coffee machine next morning. "You got laid last night, didn't you?"

I raised an eyebrow haughtily. "What on earth makes you say that?"

He cackled. "I've been people-studying for the last couple of weeks. Things I never noticed before are now becoming clearer. There's a certain smugness that goes with a truly great sexual encounter. I see it occasionally on some of our co-workers—and you have it in spades this morning."

I joined in his laughter, although I tried to make mine sound more disdainful. "You're guessing, just because I appear less miserable."

"Well, if that's what it takes to make you less of a misery, I'll pay for someone to screw you."

"You couldn't afford it," I snapped, probably with a bit more force than was necessary. The mention of getting paid to have sex hit a bad chord in my mind at that moment. "Sorry," I added when he blinked with surprise.

"I was joking," he said. "You're probably the last person I know who'd have to pay for sex. Well, you and Lewis."

"How's that going?" I asked, glad to steer the subject matter elsewhere.

"Great. He asked me to take a trip out to Palm Springs with him next weekend."

"And you said, sorry no can do, right?"

"Ha ha. Not a chance. So…" He eyed me again with suspicion. "Are you still seeing that guy you told me about?"

"Which one?"

He rolled his eyes. "The one you were at school with. You met him at your folks' place a couple of weeks ago."

"Oh, *him*." I affected disinterest. "He's okay, but you know…things happen."

I was saved from any further interrogation by William who called the office to order for our weekly meeting. *Hallelujah.*

* * * *

That night, I got another surprise. A phone call from a name and number I didn't recognize. Hector Reid. "Hello?"

"Is this Jason?"

"Yes, who's this?"

"Oh, hi, you don't know me, but I'm a friend of Simon Foster's and he told me he had a very nice time with you a couple of weeks ago. I wondered if you were available this weekend. I'm staying at the Marriott Marina. Do you know it?"

"Yes, I do. What do you have in mind?"

"Well, I thought we could spend some time together, you know, um…intimately. Are you available for that?"

Oh, boy…how do I handle this? A friend of Simon's, but this guy isn't looking for a dinner companion. At least he was upfront about what he wants me for. Can I do this?

As if sensing my hesitation, he added, "Um, Simon mentioned a fee and of course I'd be willing to meet your price, whatever it is."

My price…shit. Noah had paid me four hundred for the time I'd spent with him and Russ, so that might be a reasonable sum to ask for. "Uh, yes, that would be four hundred dollars per hour."

"Very good. I'd like at least two hours if that's all right. You do top, yes?"

"Yes, I'm versatile."

"Wonderful. Okay, I'll text you with my room number when I check in, and let's say seven p.m. I'll have room service send some food up for us, all right?"

"Perfect," I said, wondering what the hell I'd let myself in for. "Okay, Hector, I'll see you on Saturday at seven."

"I'm so looking forward to this, Jason. Bye."

"Bye." I set my phone aside and sank back on my couch. I couldn't quite believe I'd done this. Would Noah be mad at me for getting into his business? I hoped not. Could I really go through with it? Should I call Hector back and cancel? If I did it right away, maybe he could find someone else.

Shit, what have I done?

* * * *

The rest of the week I flipped and flopped on how to deal with Saturday night. By Friday I just didn't have the heart to call Hector and cancel. He'd said he was so looking forward to it, and how would he feel if I called now and begged off? *No,* I told myself, pulling on the tightest pair of jeans I owned and a loose gauzy shirt. *You're gonna do it, and you're gonna do the best job you can to make Hector enjoy his eight-hundred-dollar spree.* Nevertheless, it was with some trepidation that I set out for the hotel on Saturday night. I had packed a small bag with a change of briefs and a T-shirt, along with condoms and lube just in case Hector hadn't had the foresight to have some handy.

Parking at the Marina was a bitch, so I circled around a couple of times until I found a spot I was pretty sure I wouldn't be towed from. It was a warm, humid night and I resisted the urge to run so I wouldn't arrive at Hector's room sweaty. The hotel entry foyer was very grand and very busy. I was glad of that because I would have felt very conspicuous walking across an empty space toward the elevators. On the ride up to Hector's floor, I kept repeating what was to become my mantra in the next few weeks, *'It's about him, not me, it's about him, not me'*.

I knocked on Hector's door and took a deep breath. A few moments later the door opened to reveal a slim man in what I judged to be his late thirties, light brown hair, slightly tousled, and warm brown eyes that gazed at me with a little apprehension. He was wearing a blue button-down shirt and pressed jeans.

Hi," I said. "I'm Jason."

He stepped back so I could enter. He seemed nervous. I walked into the middle of the spacious room and dropped my bag on one of the chairs. I smiled at him and he took a tentative step toward me. *He's more nervous than me*, I thought, with a sudden surge of confidence.

"S-Simon said you were good looking, but I never expected—" He broke off and almost rushed to the bar. "W-would you like a drink?"

"If you'll join me," I replied, sounding more nonchalant than I felt.

"Of course. Scotch, bourbon, vodka?"

"Scotch please, with ice." His hands were shaking when he picked up a glass.

"Would you like me to do that?" Before he could answer, I took the glass from his hand, allowing my fingers to brush over his. Where all this effortless *savoir faire* was coming from, I had no clue. Perhaps it was his nervous attitude that made me feel as if I should take control and show him that I was the man who was going to give him the best evening of his life. I hoped that was it, anyway.

"What would you like, Hector?" I asked, throwing some ice into the glass and adding a shot of Scotch.

"Well, I love a vodka martini, but I don't know…"

"Say no more." I found a martini glass and a bottle of vermouth and proceeded to make him a martini. All the times I'd served as a bartender during my college years were now paying off. Maybe that was why I had such an affinity with bartenders, having been one myself. A dash of vermouth, a generous amount of vodka, a lemon twist and *voilà*… I handed him the glass with a bow. "Your martini, *monsieur*."

"Wow, beautiful and talented. Simon was right — you are quite the find."

Quite the find. Not something I'd been called before. I raised my glass to him. "To Simon, and to you and to a night you hopefully will remember with pleasure."

"I don't know how I ever could forget it."

Hector took a long sip of his martini, to steady his nerves, I presumed. Okay, it was time for action, and that obviously was up to me. I moved closer and bent slightly to kiss him on the mouth. His eyes widened, but after a moment he pressed back into the kiss.

"Is this your first time, Hector?"

"With someone as amazing to look at as you, yes. I've been with some men before, but, you know, mostly bar pickups. I'm not out to my family, so I have to keep in on the down low, I think they call it."

I nodded, set my drink back on the bar and began to unbutton his shirt. He had a nice chest, pale and smooth. I lowered my head and teased his left nipple, smiling at his gasp and the tremble that ran through his body.

"Drink up," I told him. "It'll help you relax."

He knocked the martini back in one gulp. "Whoa," he muttered and leaned on me. I chuckled, put an arm around him and led him over to the bed. I started to peel off my shirt. As I toed off my shoes and unbuckled my belt, he stared at me like I was the best thing he'd ever clapped eyes on. I gave my hips a little shimmy and slid my jeans slowly down my legs then tossed them aside.

"Oh wow," he whispered as I stood before him wearing the skimpiest pair of briefs that I'd found in my underwear drawer.

"Your turn," I said teasingly and finished unbuttoning his shirt. He fumbled with his belt until I took over then lowered his zipper. Dropping to my knees, I pulled his jeans down and helped him step out of them. The bulge behind his boxer briefs was enticing enough for me to run my lips over it. He moaned and thrust toward my mouth. I lowered the waistband of his briefs and licked the head of his cock. He cried out— and came all over my face. I was so surprised that I fell back on my ass.

"Oh, my God, I'm so sorry," Hector yelled and knelt in front of me staring at my jizz-covered face. I was lucky that I'd instinctively closed my eyes. That stuff can sting like hell. I grabbed him by the back of his head.

"Lick it off," I growled, using my butch voice and pulling him close enough so he could get the job done. I thought he'd struggle but instead he gave me a passable tongue bath and kept on muttering how sorry he was and how amazing I was. A guy could get carried away with all that praise. Instead, I started to laugh and when he'd finished, I kissed him.

"Been a while, has it, Hector?"

He nodded, still looking ashamed of himself. "I-I've never come so fast, but you are just so…beautiful. I'm sorry."

"Nothing to be sorry about," I said, getting to my feet and pulling him up with me. "In fact, it's kinda flattering I could get you to lose it so quickly."

He smiled and I hugged him to me and he snuggled into my arms. Later I made him a milder version of his first martini, I had another Scotch and we went to bed. He wanted me to fuck him, and I did, and he came again then fell asleep cuddling me.

So, that wasn't so bad, I mused, listening to his steady breathing. *Hector's a nice guy. Not the type I would choose to have sex with, but actually quite fun to be with. So wide-eyed and innocent, and eager to please me, regardless of the fact he's paying me. I wonder what his home life is like?*

I must have dozed off, the sex and the Scotch taking its toll. When I came to, Hector was blowing me and doing a pretty good job of it. I didn't come in his mouth and he seemed disappointed when I pulled out and sprayed over my chest. He ran a finger through my cum and licked at it.

"Nice," he murmured and smiled at me. Sweet guy.

"Mind if I shower before I go?" I asked. "You can join me if you like."

"Really?" He gave me another one of his wide-eyed gazes and leapt out of the bed, tugging at my hand to lead me to the bathroom. I gave him a blow job in the shower and he yelled loud enough to shake the tiles of the wall when he came.

Before I left, he handed me my money. "I put some more in 'cause we've gone over the two hours."

"That's sweet of you, Hector." I kissed him gently. "Call me when you're back in town?"

"Oh, you bet I will. You're the best."

"Thanks."

On my way home I figured that if there more guys like Hector, I really wouldn't mind this male escort business. Hector had paid me for three hours instead of two, and with the money I'd made with Russ and Noah and my two nights out with Simon, my savings account was swelling exponentially. I still couldn't bring myself to actually look for clients, thinking I'd be better with just the occasional referral or repeat clients like Simon and Hector…or maybe if I heard from Noah again, another three-way with him.

If I ever heard from him again.

Chapter Ten

Matt called me to say his night off this week would be Wednesday and was I available? I said I would be after I worked out. Now that I was 'quite the find,' I needed to keep up my appearance, just in case Simon or Hector sent anyone else my way. Couldn't imagine anyone asking for a flabby escort, right?

Oh hi, Hector told me you're one hot escort. I'm looking for someone who weighs at least three hundred pounds. Is that you?

No!

"So where do you work out?" Oh yeah, Matt was still on the line.

"Uh, Twenty-Four-Seven Gym on University. You know it?"

"Yeah, I'm a member. Hey, I could join you. We can spot each other. What time will you be there?"

"Five-thirty."

"Okay, and we can grab a bite to eat after, and then…"

"Gotcha." No need for him to tell me what he wanted after we ate. "Okay, see you then." Why the hell not? It had been a week since my dalliance with Hector and not a word from Noah and I was feeling horny. So again, why the hell not?

Pete called me wanting to meet for a drink. I hadn't seen him since that night at Bobby's Tavern when I mistook John the office dick's brother for the actual dick so I was happy to oblige. I asked Hank if he'd like to join us. I knew he got lonesome for Lewis during the week, their only chance to hang out and do all kinds of pornographic things to each other's bodies being at the weekends. He too was happy to oblige, so the happy threesome met at The Gallery where we could actually talk and then move on to Bobby's where we could dance and stuff.

Pete was blue because the boyfriend he'd introduced me to, Brandon, had dumped him.

"Why?" Hank wanted to know.

"Because his mother had a fit when she found out."

"That he was gay?"

"No, because he was dating a white guy."

"Oh, that's too bad."

Pete downed his drink. "Yeah, and he was dynamite in bed. Plus, he had one of the biggest—"

"Uh." I held up my hand to interrupt what I was sure was going be TMI. What was it with guys who had to brag about their boyfriends' cock size? "I'm sorry to hear about your breakup, but can we leave the size of his physical attributes out of this conversation, please?"

"What are you talking about?" Pete gave me a peeved look. "I was talking about his heart. He was so sweet and loving."

"Oh, sorry…I thought you meant something else."

"Well, the something else was pretty impressive too."

Here we go.

"I'm gonna miss it, and him."

"In that order?"

Pete smiled. The first time he'd cracked one since we sat down. "That did sound kinda shallow, I have to admit."

I was just about to signal the waiter for another round when movement by the door caught my eye. I turned to look at the two men who had just entered and I wanted the floor to open up and suck me down into the depths of whatever lay under it. Hell and its demons would be better than what was now approaching me. I could physically feel the blood leave my face, and my stomach plummet to my knees.

It was Darren and some guy...the fuck he left me for?

"Jason!" Hank took hold of my arm. "What's wrong? You look like you've seen a ghost."

"Not a ghost." Pete stared at the twosome with hostile eyes. "His ex, and maybe the guy he left Jason for."

"Oh no," Hank said weakly.

"I have to get out of here." I rose to my feet so fast I knocked my chair over, and of course every eye in the place zeroed in on me and my fucked-up clumsy move. *Kill me now, please, God. Just strike me down and smash me into a thousand tiny pieces.*

My look of shock and terror was reflected on Darren's face. Well, not the terror part. His was more shock and disdain. The fucker. The dweeb at his side was staring at me too, but without recognition. *You left me for that?* I wanted to scream. *For that pale, insipid drip of a nobody?*

What I was thinking must have been written all over my face, because Hank grabbed me and said, "Let's go, Jason," and he and Pete started dragging me toward the back exit. Outside I shook them off and leaned against the wall. I was sick to my stomach, my heart pounding as if it might burst at any moment and before I could stop myself a torrent of tears poured down my face.

"Oh dear," I heard Hank whisper through the sound of my body-wracking sobs.

"Shitfuckshit!" I yelled. "Motherfucker!

"Jason, calm down." Pete put his arms around me and Hank took my hand, patting it gently.

"Sorry, guys, sorry. I just never thought that would happen. I mean I knew it could, but I didn't think I'd react that way. Sorry."

I was babbling and they were shushing and soothing me and I felt like the most colossal fool of all time. Hank ran inside and came back out with a wad of tissues which he thrust at me.

"That's it," Pete said. "Mop up then we'll take you to Bobby's and get you shit-faced."

"I should go home."

"No, you should not." Pete shook me a little. "You're not going home in this state to sit and fester over that asshole. Okay, we won't get you shit-faced. You have to work tomorrow, but you definitely need a drink. So, let's go."

Flanked by Pete and Hank, I was led down the street to Bobby's Tavern and settled in what passed for a quiet corner if there was such a thing in that bar. I closed my eyes to shut out the happy faces of the other patrons and when I opened them again, Matt was standing there presenting me with a very large Scotch and very few rocks.

"The guys told me what happened," he said, his expression full of sympathy. "Just as well I wasn't there, or I'd have given him a bloody nose."

"Thanks," I mumbled then took a mighty gulp of the Scotch, loving the burning sensation it created on its way down inside me.

"I'd ask you to wait, but I'm not off until two," he whispered close to my ear. "Though, you're probably not in the mood right now."

I nodded. "But I'll see you tomorrow."

"Great." He kissed me on the cheek then got to his feet. "Gotta get back to work. See you guys," he told Hank and Pete and went back behind the bar.

"He's nice," Hank said.

"Yeah, he is," I agreed.

"But not for you, Jason," Pete said firmly. "He's nice and he's fun, but he's a flake. You need someone much better than that."

I wasn't in a mood to argue the point. In fact, I wasn't in the mood for anything at that moment, but another Scotch. The evening was shot, the fun we might have had yanked right out of it by the presence of *Darren fucking Anderson*.

"Was it just me or was the guy he came in with a total dweeb?" I asked them.

Hank nodded. "A total *mousy* dweeb. I'm no great shakes, but, man, that guy was drab."

"You're very cute, Hank," I told him, "and don't let anyone tell you different."

"Maybe he's a physics genius," Pete said.

"Or fabulously wealthy," Hank added.

"Yeah, that'sh gotta be it," I slurred. "Darren wouldn't give a fug about physits."

Pete grinned and Hank chuckled then we were laughing so hard I almost peed myself. "I need another drink."

"One more then I'm driving you home. I paced myself tonight 'cause I have my car."

"Yes, Mommy."

He took my hand. "You've had a shitty night, and if you need someone to stay with you tonight, I volunteer."

"That's sweet, but I'll be fine. It was just the shock, you know? It had to happen, I guess. San Diego isn't that big of a town and the gay community tends to revolve around this area. Funny, but he never really wanted to go to a gay bar when we were together. He said they were boring."

Hank arrived with my drink and I sipped it slowly. "I'm sorry about earlier, guys. Kinda ruined the evening for you both."

"That's okay," Hank said. "There will be other nights."

Pete patted my arm. "But what you said about Darren thinking gay bars are boring is interesting. Not to boost your ego too much, but why would he want to go to a gay bar when he had you?"

"Right." Hank leaned toward me. "And we're assuming the guy with him is his lover. Maybe he was just a friend, or a client."

"Oh, that's possible." I hadn't thought of that. Caught up in the horror of the moment I had, as Hank had just pointed out, assumed him to be Darren's boyfriend. Regardless, even though I'd prefer to think I hadn't been dumped for someone pale and callow like Darren's companion, it had still been an experience I never wanted repeated. My stomach hadn't fully recovered from the nausea despite the warmth of the Scotches I'd swilled down.

"Yeah, now that Hank's mentioned it, I think it's very possible we were wrong in assuming Darren's taste had hit rock bottom." Pete finished his beer. "If you're ready to go, I'll drive you home."

"I'm ready. Thanks, Peter."

"Peter? You must be drunk."

* * * *

I was slightly hungover the next morning when I awoke, but not so that I couldn't function well. Of course, the memory of seeing Darren at The Gallery was firmly lodged in my memory banks and was likely to remain there for days to come, maybe even years. Damn him all the way to hell. It would've helped if he'd looked old and decrepit, ugly and disgusting, but oh no, the fucker had looked amazing. Maybe even better than I remembered, if that were possible.

Still the same tall, athletic beauty who turned heads everywhere he went. I used to tell him he should be a fashion model instead of a lawyer, and he would smile benignly at me and kiss me gently. Now I wondered if that smile had hidden the sentiment, 'You are so full of shit, and why don't you just leave?' That was one of the hardest things for me to get over. Just how long had he been planning to drop me like a soiled tissue?

And last night…his look of shock at first then total indifference and disdain. Man, if ever I had harbored thoughts of us getting back together again, they'd been dashed by that expression. And, for just a moment the sneer had made him appear less than beautiful. After talking with Pete and Hank, it seemed more likely that the guy accompanying him wasn't his latest fuck *du jour*, but some client he was working for or friend I'd never met. It'd been obvious the guy didn't know who I was.

Coffee helped clear the cobwebs, and the shower and teeth brushing that followed got rid of any vestiges of stale booze smell before I left for the office. Hank was waiting for me at the coffee station and gave me a smile that was both wary and sympathetic.

"How d'you feel?"

"You mean after drinking too much or getting gut-punched by seeing my ex in the bar last night then breaking down like a jilted teenaged girl in front of you and Pete?"

"All of the above, I guess." He squeezed my arm. "I'm really sorry that happened to you."

I breathed out a heavy sigh. "Thanks for being so nice last night, Hank. I bet you never expected to see me making a fool of myself like that."

"It was momentous," he said with a wry smile. "I'm glad Pete was there, too. He's very nice, isn't he?"

"The best." I arched an eyebrow at him. "You're already taken."

He laughed. "I know, but I can appreciate another guy's *niceness* now and then. Can't I?"

"Of course."

"Matt seems really nice too, even though Pete thinks he's a flake."

"He's a nice flake. When you realize that about a guy, then you can't get hurt. I'm seeing him tonight, by the way."

"I could tell by the way he looked at you last night he has feelings for you."

"Fuck-buddy feelings," I said. "Which right now I am totally okay with."

Other employees started filtering into the office so we had to break off that kind of conversation and get to work.

* * * *

I didn't feel like working out, but I'd told Matt I'd meet him at the gym and it was better than going home and festering over the Darren sighting of the night before. Matt was always, at least on the occasions we'd been together, a happy guy and good company. He did approach me carefully as if weighing the odds as to whether I was going to be my usual good-natured self or a grouchy pain in the ass full of weepy recriminations against the bastard ex.

Summoning all my internal strength, I gave him a wave and a cheery hi, and he visibly relaxed and gave me a hug. "How are you?"

"Good. Yourself?"

"I'm good. Glad to see you looking better than last night."

"Let's not talk about last night, Matt. Let's talk about tonight."

He grinned and put his lips close to my ear. "I so want to fuck you tonight."

Damn me if I didn't get the start of a boner, either from the touch of his lips or from his sexy purr in my ear. "And I'm so gonna let you." I almost said, 'Let's go', but I really needed to work out. An hour or two with Matt would just be something to look forward to. A reward, and a possible salve to my body and soul. I hadn't been able to rid myself of thoughts of Darren all freaking day, and maybe Matt pounding me through the mattress would be just the ticket. *Maybe.*

"What are you working on?" he asked.

"Well, let's see, I'm sitting at the leg press…so, legs?"

"Smart ass. I'll be doing cardio for a while. See you in a few."

"Ciao." I watched him walk away and couldn't help but admire the sway of his ass atop his muscular thighs. Matt was hot without a doubt, especially in Matt's own opinion, but I couldn't fault him for that. His philosophy was *If you've got it, flaunt it.*

I concentrated on my legs for ten minutes or so then got up and wandered over to the biceps curl machine. I noticed a guy with sandy-blond hair eyeing me from the water fountain. He smiled and I smiled back. *Hey, nothing wrong with a little flirtation.* Today I needed my ego boosting, and if guys wanted to flirt, I was all up for it. He came over and stood by the machine I'd just sat at. I had to look up to get the full picture, and it was very nice indeed.

A mature man, maybe five or so years older than me and ruggedly handsome. Hazel eyes under feathered brows. His mouth was one of those I have a tendency to stare too long at, lush and made for me to kiss. My face grew warm at the thought and I felt a definite stirring in my groin. I concentrated instead on his muscled arms and chest which provided no distraction at all from my carnal thoughts. They were a sight to savor and maybe even caress, if I had enough nerve, which I didn't.

"Hi," he said and sat down on the machine next to me. "I haven't seen you here before."

"I don't come often enough," I replied, smiling. "But I've decided to start a new regimen, and here I am. I'm Jason, by the way."

"David Farmer." He held out his hand and I gripped it, liking the dryness of his palm even though the rest of him was covered in a fine sheen of sweat. "Are you available for a coffee or something stronger after your workout?"

"Sorry, no. I'm with him tonight." I pointed at where Matt was trying to destroy the treadmill he was using like a racetrack. "I'll take a raincheck, though."

He nodded. "You have your cell on you?"

I pulled it from my shorts. "Wouldn't be caught dead without it." We traded numbers then talked for a few more minutes. I found out he was the managing director of a loan company in Mission Valley, lived in Mission Hills and had only moved to San Diego three months ago.

"So, I'm trying to make new friends," he said, his hazel eyes twinkling. "And you look friendly."

"I am." I grinned up at him. "Call me and we can go for a drink or something."

"I will." We both watched as Matt headed our way, wiping sweat from his face and chest. "Bye, Jason. Nice meeting you."

"You too."

"Who was that?" Matt asked. Was there a hint of jealousy in his tone?

"David," I replied, and started my biceps curls routine.

"You know him?" He sat astride the machine next to me after adjusting the weights.

"I do now."

"He was trying to pick you up?"

"I guess. He seems nice…new in town and looking to hook up, make friends, that kind of thing."

"Huh. What did you tell him?"

"I said I was with you, tonight." I omitted the fact that David and I had traded phone numbers.

Our workouts over, Matt and I showered, separately of course. The gym, although in the liberal part of San Diego, still doesn't approve of boys co-mingling in the shower room for some hanky-panky. Afterward we walked over to the Happy Grill across the street for a snack then on to my place for a different kind of snack.

Matt was, like always, full steam ahead, and tonight he was everything I needed…a bit rough and demanding. I only pretended to resist him when he flung my legs over his shoulders without much in the way of foreplay. He fucked me like he too was trying to forget something or someone, and I welcomed the almost desperate kisses he rained over my face and throat as he came. Thoroughly drained, we lay in each other's arms until we were ready to go again.

"Wanna fuck me, Jason?" Matt whispered in my ear.

I gave him a surprised look. I hadn't considered he'd want to bottom for me. "I'd love to," I said, and he grinned.

"I know you've been thinking I'm strictly top, but I like to flip-flop now and then. It makes me feel…"

He didn't finish but I caught the vulnerable expression that flitted over his face and I kissed him gently. "Wanted, right?" I murmured.

He nodded. "Sometimes when it's all over, I get an emptiness inside me, as if the guy I'm with just sees me like I'm some fuck machine, you know? Not you," he added quickly. "You're always sweet afterward, and you talk to me like we're boyfriends not just fuck buddies. You're a nice guy, Jason."

Hank's words from the other night came back to me. *'I could tell by the way he looked at you he has feelings for you.'* I brushed that away quickly. I was not going to get involved with Matt any further than we already were.

"You are too, Matt, and now that we have this mutual admiration society going, I am going to fuck you till you scream." I figured a quick return to the previous subject was safer than continuing a conversation that might get awkward. He growled something then got on his hands and knees and presented his fairly spectacular ass to me. I reached for a condom and the bottle of lube. Once I got him ready by using my fingers to stretch him a little, I sheathed myself and entered him. Slowly at first. I didn't know how often Matt allowed this, but he seemed pretty tight.

"Okay?" I asked and he grunted and pushed his ass toward me. I thrust home and he groaned and clamped down on the base of my cock.

"Move, Jason," he ground out. "Fuck me like you mean it, till I scream like you said I would."

I gripped his hips, pulled out then rammed my way back inside him. Again and again, I pounded into him, our moans filling the air around us, that and the slapping sound of flesh on flesh were all I could hear. He reared up suddenly, anchoring himself on my lap, forcing me farther inside him. I wrapped an arm around him, holding him against my chest while I gripped his throbbing erection and pumped it to the rapid rhythm our bodies had found. He turned his face to mine, seeking a kiss, and I covered his lips with mine, thrusting my tongue into his waiting mouth. The

J.P. Bowie

visceral sensation of our tongues tangling made even this awkward position thrilling.

Drenched in sweat, we rocked together, every upward heave of my hips met by him writhing down over my cock. I knew from the way my breathing was becoming more and more labored I was ready to explode. I could tell he was almost there too by the moans and whimpers he fed into my mouth. He covered my hand holding his erection, as if to speed up his climax.

"Oh, shit, Jason….oh, fuck, I'm coming." And he did, his cum arcing through my fingers, his body taut as steel against mine. He fell forward and I followed, driving myself into him while my orgasm raced through me, exploding into the condom so deep inside him.

We lay in a tangled, sweaty heap. I pressed my lips to his neck, my mind no more than a starry but empty space, devoid of thoughts if only for a minute or two.

When I could speak, I said, "You didn't scream."

His chuckle came from deep in his chest. "I did inside my head. That was fantastic, Jason. I knew you'd do it right."

Do it right. Praise indeed.

Chapter Eleven

I received a call from Noah two days later. I could tell from the careful way he approached our conversation that this wasn't an entirely social call.

"Are you free over the weekend?" he asked after we'd exchanged a few pleasantries.

"This weekend?"

"Yes, I have a proposition for you. Simon told me his friend Hector was delighted with you and couldn't wait to see you again. I wondered if you'd be up for something similar."

I chuckled. "Similar?"

"Similar as in a friend of Simon's."

"He has a lot of friends," I exclaimed, laughing.

"He does. But this guy is his nephew."

"What?"

"Yeah. He came out to Simon only a couple of weeks ago. He's thirty and has never been with a man."

"Wow."

"Yeah, I know, hard to believe in this day and age, but there it is. He told Simon he wants to be with a man but he gets cold feet whenever anyone approaches him."

"Poor guy, but I have a question. Why me and not you? Simon knows you so much better and thinks highly of you."

"Well, for starters, Eric — that's his nephew's name — lives in San Diego and this weekend I have a full schedule, so I couldn't fit him in."

He has a full schedule. Boy, do I not belong in this guy's life…

"What's he look like?"

"I have no idea, but I'd say, if he's related to Simon, chances are he's no troll."

"And that was completely shallow of me, wasn't it?"

He laughed lightly. "A bit, but hey, if there's sex involved you have a right to wonder…and if he acts like an asshole you have the right to walk away."

"Really? Good to know."

"But again, I don't think Simon would send him to you if he was a jerk. It's up to you, Jason. Do I tell Simon it's okay to give Eric your phone number, or not?"

"Yeah, it's okay. And I promise I'll be gentle."

He laughed again. "That's sweet. Oh, just one more thing. Payment will be coming from Simon, not Eric. He doesn't want the guy to think he's dealing with an escort. He wants him to have the full 'boyfriend experience'. I mean, he'll know of course, but he won't have to hand over the money at the end."

"Simon is the best," I said.

"Yes, he is. Okay, Jason. You should hear from Eric in the next couple of days."

"Oh, should I have him come to my place or offer to go to his?"

"Why don't you ask him? He might have a roommate which could make him feel uncomfortable."

"Oh, right. Okay, I'll give him the choice."

"Good. Gotta go, Jason. Thanks for doing this. I hope we can get together again soon. Bye."

"Me too. Bye, Noah." I sighed after I ended the call. His hoping we could get together soon wasn't exactly a pledge. And like I'd thought earlier when he mentioned his 'full schedule' just how much room was there for me in his life?

After work the following day I forced myself to go to the gym. If I was going to get repeat calls from Noah or Simon, I'd best be in the best shape possible, was my reasoning. I was pretty toned but there was always room for improvement as they say, and an hour a day working out wasn't that much of a chore. Of course, right in the middle of me lifting some free weights, my cell phone chimed.

A text from Eric, Simon's nephew, giving me his phone number and the message, *Please call me.* I don't know why, but those three words got to me. They made me sad, for God only knew what reason. I didn't quite get it. Maybe he was too nervous to call me himself? The guy was thirty years old, not a kid, but some guys could be short on self-confidence even at that age. I mean, what about that melt-down I had a few nights ago, just because Darren walked into the same bar I was sitting in, enjoying a drink with friends? No, it didn't take much to put a hole in one's ego.

I punched in his number.

"Hello?" The voice sounded young and nervous. I paused before answering. Should I go for a hale and hearty "Hi!" or a well-modulated and smooth, "Hi, Eric, this is Jason"? I opted for the latter choice. The other might scare him into thinking I'm some over-the-top twit full of forced jocularity.

"Oh, hi." He sounded a little more relaxed. Seemed the smooth approach had been the right choice.

"How are you?"

"I-I'm good, thanks. Are you calling because of my Uncle Simon's suggestion?"

"No, I'm calling because you sent me a text asking me to call you."

"Oh, right. But you are the Jason my uncle told me about?"

"Yep, that's me. He thought we should get together. How d'you feel about that?"

"I-I think I'd like that. Did he tell you I-I haven't been with anyone before…in that manner, I mean?"

I smiled. This one was even more innocent than Hector. "Yes, he intimated that. I can assure you, you'll be perfectly safe with me. Nothing will happen that you don't want."

"O-okay, good. I'm kinda nervous."

No kidding. "That's fine. I think everyone is nervous first time around."

"Were you?"

"Nervous like a cat in a room full of rocking chairs."

He laughed. A nice sound. "I haven't heard that one before."

"So, Eric…your place or mine?"

"Would you mind if I came to your place?"

"Not at all. Here's the address." I reeled it off for him and repeated it when he asked me to. "It's right off Adams. Make the left turn on Westminster. There's parking out front."

"Okay. I-I'm looking forward to meeting you, Jason."

"Likewise. I'll see you Saturday at say…eight?"

"Yes, bye."

"Bye." I sat looking at my phone for a few moments wondering how the hell I was going to make this shy man have the time of his life. Then I remembered Noah's words, *'Just be yourself, Jason. He'll love you'*.

Right.

As luck would have it, David, the guy I'd met in the gym a couple of days before, called me asking if I had anything planned for Saturday night. *Well, dammit.*

"'Fraid so," I told him with a twinge of regret. "I'm meeting a friend. Another raincheck?"

"You're a popular guy," he said and I could hear a trace of disappointment in his voice. "Okay, I'll give you a call next week?"

"I'm sure we can connect at some point," I replied cheerfully, but wondered why he didn't mention the possibility of tonight. "Are you busy this evening?"

"My sister's in town. She wanted to check out San Diego because I've been pretty enthusiastic about it since I moved here."

"Where did you live before?"

"Sacramento. The company transferred me to take over the branch here. So far, I'm enjoying it. I'd really like to see you, Jason. Maybe we could plan on a night next week?"

"Sure, I'd like that."

"I'm out of town for a meeting, leaving Sunday, back Wednesday. How about Thursday? I'll take you to dinner."

"Sounds great, but we'll go Dutch, okay?"

He chuckled. "We'll argue about that later. I'll call you when I get back and we can fix a time."

"All right. Have a safe trip, David."

"Thanks. Take care of yourself until I get back."

I was smiling when I hung up. It had been nice talking to David, and the thought of a dinner date with him was more than a little exciting. And it would be a *normal* date with maybe just a goodnight kiss at the end. The next date maybe we'd get to second base...and then... I laughed to myself. Who was I kidding? If he wanted sex after dinner, I'd be all up for that!

Was it then that I started thinking like a slut?

Saturday, I cleaned the apartment top to bottom, changed the sheets and prettied the place up with a couple of flowering plants from the local supermarket. I also bought some beer and wine just in case Eric needed loosening up a little. I spent an hour at the gym then got my hair cut. Hank had told me it was cute the way it curled up at the back of my neck, but it was also a bit girly. That boy was really coming out of his shell. A couple of months ago, he wouldn't have said boo to me. Now he was my hairstyle critic?

I called my folks when I got back to the apartment. My mom always sounded surprised when I called even though Saturday was our telephone day.

"How are you, darling?" she asked, on a gasp.

"Fine. You sound out of breath. Are you all right?"

"Oh yes. It's always a surprise to hear your voice."

"Mom, I call you every Saturday. Why are you shocked?"

"Not shocked, dear. Surprised."

I gave up. "Anyway, what's new at the Harrison residence? How's Dad?"

"Busy gardening as usual. Noah came over this morning to give him a hand."

He did? "He did? Th-that was nice of him."

"Yes. He asked if we'd heard from you. I said no."

"Mom! You know perfectly well I call you on Saturdays. Why did you tell him you hadn't heard from me?"

"Because I hadn't until now," she replied sweetly.

"Did he ask how I was?" *Needy…*

"Yes, he said he really wanted to visit you sometime, but he has such a full schedule it's difficult for him to get away."

Yeah, that fucking full schedule again. Why does it bug me so much?

I steered the conversation away from Noah and for a while Mom chattered on about her social work and the neighbors who keep asking how I am and when am I getting married.

"*Married?* I thought they knew about me."

"They do dear, but you know how people are — they don't quite believe it, even when I say you haven't snagged the right man yet."

My mom. No one finer in the whole dang world.

My doorbell rang at exactly eight o'clock. *Punctual fellow.* I took a deep breath and opened the door and stared at the blond giant on my doorstep. *Holy crap, he's got to be at least six-five.* There weren't many guys I had to crane my neck in order to focus on the face, but here he was, the living example of just that.

"Jason?" That young and nervous voice was so at odds with his appearance. Not only was he tall, he was built and he was beautiful. How in hell had he escaped being propositioned on a daily or even hourly basis for thirty years? Well, twenty maybe, once he got past puberty.

"Yeah, come on in, Eric." I gave him a big welcoming smile and he smiled back and took the hand I offered in his big mitt. Wow. Was this another Lewis who was big—everywhere? Well, at some point or another, I was going to find out. I pulled him into a hug, no easy task. He had to have thirty pounds on me at least. He stayed stiff as a tree trunk and didn't put his arms around me. *Okay, not the hugging kind.* I stepped back and clapped him on his denim-clad arm. It was difficult to not notice how hard his biceps were.

"So, can I get you a drink, beer, wine?"

"A beer, please."

Oh good, that gave me something to do other than stare at him and wonder what the hell I'd gotten myself into. I grabbed a couple of cans from the fridge.

"You're very good-looking," he said, watching me pop a can for him.

"Thanks. You are too. Would you like a glass?"

"No, the can is fine." We both took long swallows then he cast an appraising look around the living room, his blue-eyed gaze lingering on the door that led to the bedroom. "You live here alone?"

"Oh yes. How about you? You have a roommate?"

He shook his head, his blond hair falling over his brow. He shoved it back impatiently. "So, how do we do this?" he asked after knocking back the rest of his beer.

"Well, usually I start out by holding and kissing my cl—uh, guest." I'd almost said *client*, and somehow that didn't seem quite right. "Would you like me to kiss you?"

"I've never kissed a man before…I mean on the lips. I have kissed my father and my Uncle Simon, but just on the cheek."

I finished my beer then put the can aside and walked toward him. "Bend toward me," I told him. He did and I put my hands on his wide shoulders and kissed his lips. He didn't kiss me back. "Okay?" He nodded so I kissed him again, this time a little more firmly and ran the tip of my tongue over his plump lower lip. He started and his lips parted in seeming surprise. I didn't push my tongue inside his mouth, but let the tip linger, waiting for his reaction.

He put his hands on my waist and pulled me in closer and I chose that moment to deepen our kiss, sliding a hand behind his head to hold him steady. He whimpered softly, his tongue meeting mine, and the whimper became a moan. I pulled back and took his hand.

"Let's sit on the couch," I said, leading him to it. "That way, we'll be more of each other's height."

"Yes, sorry, I am awkward."

"Not awkward, just tall." We sat and I kissed him again. "Remember, if I do something you don't like, tell me right away. Don't just suffer in silence. I want you to enjoy this, okay?"

He nodded. "So far, I'm enjoying it," he said with a shy smile.

"Good." I stroked his smoothly shaven cheek. "You smell nice, you look great. Why don't you have a boyfriend?"

He ducked his head and sighed. "I've tried. I just don't have it in me to go to a bar or a place where there's a bunch of people. You've no idea how many times I've loitered outside the gay bars on University and just can't make myself take that first step inside."

"Gay bars can be intimidating at times. You don't have any gay friends you could go with?"

He shook his head.

"Have you tried an online dating site?"

"I've hooked up online a couple of times, but when they want to fix a date for us to meet, I just chicken out. Stupid, huh?"

"And yet you came here tonight. You didn't chicken out."

"I guess I'm getting desperate."

I laughed. "Oh, such a smooth talker."

He blushed. "Sorry, I didn't mean it that way."

I grabbed his hand and kissed it. "I know you didn't. C'mere…" I wrapped my arms around him and he reciprocated, holding me tight against his broad chest. I nuzzled his neck, his ear, then trailed my lips over his jawline before laying a long, really deep kiss on his mouth. After unbuttoning the denim shirt he was wearing, I slipped a hand inside and teased his left nipple between my thumb and forefinger. His body bucked and he gasped into my mouth. I ran my hand further down his muscled torso. He really was built and his skin was soft and smooth. Quite the prize, and once again I wondered why no one had snapped him up long ago, regardless of his shyness.

He gripped my hand when I started to unbuckle his belt. "It's okay," I murmured on his lips and carried on until I had it undone then started working on his button fly. There's something really sexy about button flies. A zipper is easy to yank down, metal buttons take longer, allowing the anticipation to grow as well as what's behind the fly. I could feel his hardness against my knuckles and hear his breath quicken inside his chest.

I slid off the couch until I was kneeling between his sturdy thighs. Before I went any further, I looked up at him with a questioning smile. "Okay?"

"Yes," he choked out and raised his hips when I started to pull his jeans and briefs down. His cock sprang out hot and hard. Not as big as I expected from a man his size, but nice nevertheless, with a girth that would satisfy any mouth or ass. I licked the head and murmured my approval when his pre-cum slicked my tongue.

"Nice," I whispered, gazing up at him, and he stared back at me like he couldn't quite believe this was happening. He laid a hand on my head but didn't exert any pressure as I went down on his cock, sliding my lips from the tip to the base with one long, smooth motion that brought a moan from deep inside him. His cock pulsed in my mouth and more pre-cum spilled from it, the tangy taste making my own cock hard as a baseball bat. It seemed crazy to me that this guy was paying me for doing this when, if I'd met him in a bar or an online dating site, I'd have been happy to have sex with such a beautiful man for free!

I massaged his naked thighs while I sucked, then quickened the pace a little. I worked one hand under his balls to tease his taint with my fingers. His body shuddered and he gripped the hair on my head as he jerked upward with a hoarse cry. His cum flooded my mouth, a torrent I almost choked on but managed to swallow, and I continued to suck until he was writhing under me and babbling about *oh God, how amazing is this* and other stuff I couldn't understand. I held him there until the last drop was squeezed from him and he slumped back against the couch cushions.

When I released him and looked up, his expression was one of total pleasure, his lips slightly parted in a smile, his eyes glazed and slightly unfocussed. I scooted up over his body and kissed him, pushing my tongue into his mouth, letting him taste his own cum. He put his arms around me and crushed me in an embrace as if he'd never let me go. I knew this had to have been a moment for him, something he'd possibly dreamed of, thought of, worried about for years, and I just hoped that he felt some kind of fulfillment now that he'd experienced at least some of the things men do together.

"Okay?" I murmured.

"God yes, Jason. So much more than okay. I mean, I've watched guys do this on videos and imagined how it would feel, but you made it so much more, so incredible." He stroked my face gently. "Can I do it for you? I'd really like to know what it's like."

"Sure, but let's get a little more comfortable. How about we do it on the bed?"

Chapter Twelve

I got to my feet then pulled him up off the couch. Standing, he towered over me again. His jeans and briefs were still around his ankles and his shirt was wide open, showing a slightly sweaty chest. I knelt down and removed his cowboy boots and had him step out of his jeans then took his hand and led him into the bedroom. I had prepped it a bit with a couple of candles, and some soft music playing. After I turned back the comforter and top sheet, I slipped off his shirt and threw it over a chair. Naked, he was magnificent and I wondered if I'd always be this lucky with the guys Noah sent me.

"You still have all your clothes on," he said, stating the obvious.

"Why don't you remedy that?" I held up my arms so he could pull my T-shirt up and over my head while I toed of my sneakers and shimmied out of my jeans. His gaze zeroed in on the bulge in my briefs and he reached out a tentative hand to touch it. I took his hand and pressed it against my crotch and he visibly shuddered. He sat down heavily on the edge of the bed and I straddled him. He fell back with me on top of him. My cock was still safely covered so I inched myself forward over his chest until, if he wanted to, he could touch it again, or if he got bolder, put his mouth around it.

He surprised me by lowering the waistband and taking my erection out. For a few moments he stared at it as if wondering if he had the nerve to do what I'd done for him—then he licked the glistening head. Some things can't be controlled, and his licking action caused a spurt of my pre-cum to land on his tongue. I flinched, thinking he might be disgusted, but he seemed to savor it. His eyes gleamed and he smiled.

"Do I taste as good as you?" he asked guilelessly.

"Better, I think." I leaned toward his mouth and kissed him "Has anyone ever told you you're adorable?"

"I can't think of a one."

"Well, let me be the first of which I am sure there will be many."

"Can I suck you now?" Was that impatience in his tone? Truly adorable. I rolled off him and tugged him onto the bed properly. He came willingly or I'd have been tugging all night without moving him an inch.

I lay on my side with my face in his crotch and my cock within easy reach of his mouth. I'd let him find his own way there in his own time while I pleasured him some more. It wasn't long before a definite wet swipe of his tongue got my attention. It gave me just the tiniest, smuggest thrill that mine was the first cock he'd ever got close to, and from the way he was now lapping at it, however inexperienced, it felt and sounded like he was enjoying himself. I gave his the attention it deserved. It was already hard and throbbing in my mouth and my swirling tongue up and down its thick length had him moaning and sucking me with gusto. I fought the urge to come, unsure of how he'd react to a mouthful of my semen, but when I started to ease out, he clamped his hands on my butt and held me while he sucked harder.

I knew from my own experience there was a certain thrill of the unknown the first time I swallowed another guy's load. My first time was with Darren and I was so in love with him I would have accepted anything he wanted to do with, or to, me. But this was certainly the wrong fucking time to be thinking of that jerk-off, so I clouded my mind and concentrated on taking Eric to the threshold of Heaven. Yeah, OTT, but I wanted this to be good for him, so good that he'd want to do it over and over, with other guys, of course.

He came first, filling my mouth again, which, as he'd come only a half hour or so ago, was pretty impressive. Unable to ignore the thrilling tingles that engulfed my groin and thighs, I let go and heard him gag, and thought, *Oh shit*, but he didn't pull back and kept his hands on my butt, holding me in place.

When we finally rolled apart and I scooted up to give him a reward in the way of a kiss, he was smiling at me. A good sign. A *really* good sign. He returned my kiss and we traded the vestiges of our cum, still on our tongues. He seemed happy, and that made me feel as if I'd done something worthwhile. It could be argued that I'd done no such thing, that instead I'd led him to the brink of debauchery, but when our kiss ended and he said, "I am so glad my first time was with you," all my doubts were dispelled.

He laid his head on my chest and within minutes he was fast asleep. Coming twice in a short space of time can do that to a guy and I was glad he felt relaxed enough with me to snooze for a time. I wondered if he'd want to take the next step. Anal sex isn't everyone's delight, and having taken so long to get his far, it just might be too much, but I would let him fuck me if he wanted to go that route. He slept for a time and I must've dozed off myself only to be startled awake when Eric sat up suddenly and yelped.

I took his hand. "Hey, it's okay. You just got a bit disoriented. You're with me…Jason."

"Oh God, sorry. Jeez, you must think I'm an idiot."

"Not at all. I'm guessing you're not used to waking up with a strange man in a strange bed."

He chuckled and fell back on the pillow. "You're right. Sorry I passed out."

"No problem," I said and he put his arm across my chest and kissed my shoulder.

"I feel so comfortable with you, Jason."

"Thanks, that was my goal, to make this enjoyable for you so that you'll want to do it again, and with someone you're attracted to."

"I still don't think I could make the first move."

"You might not have to. Hey, I have a wild idea." I sat up and leaned on my elbow so I could look down at him. "What if you and I go out to, say…Bobby's Tavern. This would be totally nothing to do with what your uncle arranged. Just two buds out for fun. Bobby's has a happy hour, Sundays at four. You'll get to experience a gay bar, and I'll be there to make sure you don't get into any trouble…unless you want to, of course." I grinned and waggled my eyebrows to make sure he knew I was joking. "What d'you say?"

He gazed up at me with those big blue eyes of his and nodded slightly. "I-I think I could do it if I were there with you."

"I'll stay glued to your side, although that might not be a good idea should someone show more than just a passing interest in you." I grinned again. "But I can step aside at the right moment. There'll be dancing. Do you dance?"

"Actually, yes. I enjoy it."

"Good. So it's a date. Tomorrow at four, I'll meet you outside Bobby's Tavern. Okay?"

"Okay." Shyly, he pulled me down for a kiss and I let my lips linger on his until he opened and let me in. We kissed for a long time and I could feel him grow hard against my thigh. I figured it was time for my next move.

"Would you like to fuck me, Eric?"

His eyes grew wide as he stared at me. "I-I've only ever fucked once… It was a girl in college…years ago."

Jesus, you poor guy.

"I-I might make a mess of it."

"No, you won't. Here's what we're gonna do… Wait, would you like to shower first?"

He nodded so fast I guessed he was thinking it would help stall for time before the *deed*. I rolled off the bed and held out my hand, which he took as if I'd handed him a lifeline. I led him to the bathroom, really glad that it had a walk-in shower instead of those rickety plastic tubs in so many apartments. He was a big man, and we needed space for the two of us. I turned on the water and stepped in, holding out my hand for him again. Once he was in beside me, I grabbed the sponge and bodywash and started to give his chest and abs my total attention.

"Turn around." He did so and I lathered the broad expanse of his back then passed the sponge over his beautiful butt. Using some foam, I slipped my fingers into his crack and lightly circled his hole. He gasped and pushed back into my touch. I slid one finger past his resistance far enough to tease his prostate and he groaned and pulled away. He turned to face me.

"I think I'd rather you fucked me." His voice was thick with perhaps apprehension mixed with emotion.

"Okay." I quickly ran the sponge over my body and we rinsed off together. I handed him a towel once we'd stepped out of the shower. I watched him carefully while we dried each other. If he showed any sign that he'd regretted what he'd said, I'd make it easy on him by offering to let him fuck me instead.

We got back on the bed and I grabbed the lube and condoms from the nightstand drawer and laid them on the sheet beside us. "Easiest way is on your hands and knees," I told him, and he immediately assumed the position. I knelt behind him and took a moment to admire what a lot of guys were missing, if they only knew it. Twin globes of muscular flesh, covered in the smoothest of skin. And all mine to enjoy. I lowered my face to this fine ass. He grunted in surprise when I ran my tongue between his butt-cheeks. I knew with a certainty that this was something he'd never have experienced before, and again not all guys went for it, but from the way he was wriggling his hot ass over my tongue, I was pretty sure he was enjoying it.

I inserted a finger alongside my tongue and he moaned and mumbled something I couldn't make out. "What, Eric?"

"I wish I could see you. This is nice, but I like looking at you, too."

"We can do that." I squirted a heap of lube on my fingers and got him ready. He flinched when the cold gel touched his anus and I pushed one then two fingers inside him. I sheathed myself quickly and flopped down beside him. "You are going to straddle me, okay?"

"Okay." He sat astride me and I guided my cock to his entrance.

"Now, you're going to control this, Eric. Hold my erection and sit back on it. Take as much as you want at first. If there's pain, stop until it recedes."

From where I was lying, the view was amazing. Eric was every gay man's wet dream. His face with those limpid blue eyes and pouty mouth, his chest and torso, so deftly sculpted into mouth-watering planes of smooth muscle…all of him, perfection, and I was the lucky so-and-so who got to enjoy every inch of him tonight. I ran my hands over his chest and abs, encouraging him to take this first plunge of what he so clearly wanted. He grimaced a little when the broad head of my cock breached his ass muscles, but he didn't stop, shifting slightly to accommodate more of me. He took his hand away from the base of my dick and sat back with a sound that was part groan, part snarl. Yeah, the burn had been there, but he was eager to feel all of my thick length inside him—and what was pain when pleasure lay ahead?

He gasped and gazed down at me, his face flushed, his lips slightly parted as he began to move up and down on my straining shaft. I lifted my hips to go deeper and he grabbed my hands and held them to his chest while he rode me.

"Yesss…" It was almost a sigh that hissed from his lips and I arched myself up to him so we could share a kiss. "Oh, my God, Jason, this is more than I thought it could be. It could never be this good again."

"Yes, it could and it will," I said fervently. "The first time is always something you'll remember, but with the man you will meet and love, it will be all the more amazing, believe me."

It took a bit of doing, but I managed to topple him over onto his side without breaking our union. Face to face I began to fuck him in earnest and he clung to me as our bodies writhed together, meeting every thrust from me with his own. It was amazing for me too, the total surrender of this big, beautiful man in my arms. I squeezed a hand into the space our sweat-slicked torsos afforded so I could grip his raging erection and bring him to the edge along with me.

"Jason," he groaned and his hot cum sprayed between our chests and his body bucked and shuddered in the throes of his climax. Two more ramming thrusts and I couldn't hold on any longer. I came hard into the condom, so hard and fast that I saw stars. We clung together as we came down from the heights of orgasmic bliss—at least that was how it felt for me—and from the way Eric was rambling and covering my face and lips with wet kisses, I was sure he was right there with me, reveling in it just as I had.

After a while I rolled off the bed, removed the condom and went to the bathroom to dispose of it. I ran a wet washcloth over my chest then rinsed it and took it back to where Eric lay, flushed and silent on the bed. I wiped his chest, and he stared up at me with an unreadable expression.

Oh, Lord, is he regretting this whole thing? Is he wishing he'd never agreed to any of this?

"Eric, are you all right?"

"Yes, just a bit dazed. Can I ask you something?"

"Of course." I passed the washcloth over his cock and he jumped. "Sorry, still sensitive?"

"Did you enjoy any of that?" he asked, instead of answering me. "Or was it just what you thought I needed?"

"You're not very observant," I said, tapping the tip of his nose.

"How'd you mean?"

"Men can't usually fake orgasms and I can assure you mine was a doozy." I bent to kiss his lips. "Don't sell yourself short, Eric. You are a very desirable man, and this evening has been a total pleasure for me."

"I can't even begin to tell you how much I've loved being here with you." He took my hand and kissed it. "Can I see you again?"

"You're seeing me tomorrow at Bobby's Tavern, remember?"

"I remember, but I meant for another night like this."

I met his gaze and hesitated. Did he know what that meant? I didn't want to crush his feelings, but he had to realize what this had been.

"I-I know I have to pay, and I'm okay with that."

"Oh, Eric, you don't need to do this. You're a gorgeous man. It's hard for me to believe you haven't found the love of your life, but you will, I know you will."

He sighed then give me a little smile. "Okay, but until then, can I see you like...like this?"

I nodded. "Yes, it will be my pleasure as well as yours. But I want you to promise you'll get out more often, go where you might meet someone looking for you."

He reached up and caressed my lips with his fingertips. "I could fall in love with you."

"Please don't do that. I want to see you fall in love with someone who deserves you."

"Someone broke your heart, am I right?"

What is he – a psychic? "We'll talk about that some other time," I said softly and kissed his cheek.

"Okay." He got out of the bed and started to dress. "I hope my uncle is paying you top dollar."

"Let's not talk about that."

"I'll ask him so I don't short-change you when I come see you again."

"*Eric…*"

"*Jason.*" He grinned and hugged me tight. "G'bye. Don't stand me up tomorrow."

"As if. See you tomorrow."

Chapter Thirteen

Noah called me Sunday morning. I experienced a tiny twinge of annoyance that he was checking up on my performance, if I was right about the reason for the call. However, he surprised me by chatting about visiting my mom and dad and helping Dad in the garden.

"Yeah, Mom said you'd been by."

"They've both been so good to me over the years," he said. "After my mother died, I lived with my Aunt Peggy. She knew your mom from the charity work they all did, so I'd see them quite often."

"That's great. I know they're very fond of you."

"And I am of them. Anyway, Jason, how'd it go with Eric?"

"You know, I cannot believe that guy is single. He's shy and sexually naïve but, Noah, he is gorgeous. He should have men panting after him every time he goes out. He was a delight to lead into the joy of gay sex," I added with a chuckle. "Simon should've got him a copy of that book."

"Obviously, he liked you, right?"

"Yes, I think maybe a little too much, but I'm going to lead him in the right direction to find a real boyfriend. I'm taking him to Bobby's Tavern this afternoon so he can experience a bar full of gay men. He told me he's never been to one, so this should get him over his fear of flying solo, if you know what I mean."

"Jason, I don't know if that's such a good idea. You said you thought he was maybe too fond of you already. He might be imagining this is a date. You have to learn to treat clients as what they are, just clients. They're not going to be your friends."

I was quiet for a few moments, not liking his tone. "It's not a date," I said frostily. "It's this one time to get him into the gay scene that he's dying to be a part of, but is too shy to take the first step. All I'm doing is being there so he'll feel less intimidated. He asked me if he could see me again...for sex...and told me he knew he'd have to pay me. He understands the situation, Noah. He's not stupid."

"I'm not inferring he is, Jason, but you must understand the situation too."

My blood began to boil. *Who the fuck does he think he's talking to?*

"Clients cannot be your friends, Jason," he continued. "If you allow that to happen, they will expect favors from you without a fee. It's really nice that you want to take care of Eric, but you mustn't let it become a habit. I don't meet any of my clients off the books. Not even for a coffee. And, quite honestly, I don't think they'd ever expect that of me."

Well, fuck. That had left me with a sour taste in my mouth, and I didn't have a clue about how I should respond.

"Jason?"

"Yeah, okay, I get it," I said, my voice flat. "But I'm not canceling on him today. The guy's ego is too fragile for a letdown so soon after an invitation. I'll explain to him the male escort philosophy so he doesn't get the wrong idea."

"Jason, I'm sorry if you're upset." Noah had obviously decided to ignore my male escort philosophy dig. *His* voice was even and smooth as always. "I just wanted to make sure you understand the difficulties you will encounter should you become too friendly with your clients."

"Like I said, I got it. I'll be a good boy in future."

I heard him sigh, but I was still pissed at his reaction. Maybe this male escort thing wasn't for me after all, and suddenly the thought of having a three-way with Noah and that Russ guy just wasn't as appealing anymore. Time to cut the call.

"Okay, Noah, good talking to you. I'll take care of things this afternoon."

"Bye, Jason."

I hung up feeling shitty, and hoped Noah did too. I had a feeling I wouldn't be hearing from him quite so much and probably no recommendations would be coming my way. Well, I'd lived without them before. I could do it again.

* * * *

When I saw Eric standing outside Bobby's Tavern, it put a big smile on my face. It was a beautiful, warm San

Diego day and he was dressed appropriately in a yellow shirt and white shorts, the ensemble looking great against his tan and his blond hair. I was wearing a blue tee and khaki shorts and had decided to walk the couple of miles from my apartment as the weather was so good.

He smiled and waved when he saw me and I was quick to notice all the heads that were turned in his direction as guys passed him on the street. He was a beauty and I was determined he'd meet the 'right guy' — if not today, then soon. And screw what Noah had told me.

"Hi!" I gave him a big hug and was glad when he hugged me back.

"Hi, Jason." His face was a tad flushed. Excitement, embarrassment? I wasn't sure but I took his hand and led him into the bar's interior. I'd expected all eyes to be on him, and as we walked up to the bar to place our orders, I was proven right.

"What'll it be, handsome?" The bartender, not Matt, gazed at Eric with just the right amount of awe and lust in his eyes.

I chuckled. "Beer, Eric?"

He nodded. "You have draft Stella?"

"Brewed especially for you, Eric," the bartender replied with a smile and a wink. I didn't know this one, but he was a charmer.

"I'll have the same," I told him then added, "What's your name?"

"Steve. And you are?"

"Jason, and you already know Eric."

"Not well enough, but I hope to remedy that."

I glanced up at Eric. His face had taken on an interesting shade of pink and he seemed to be transfixed, staring at Steve as if he were some rare species he never seen before. The guy had a few things in his favor. One, he was way over six feet. Not as tall as Eric but had to be at least six-three. A definite advantage over we lesser mortals.

"He's cute, right?" I said when Steve moved away to get our drinks.

"Y-you think he's interested in me?" Eric stammered.

"Honey, everyone in here with a pulse is interested in you. Take a look around the bar. You'll see what I'm talking about."

With his height advantage, he had no problem seeing over the heads of the other patrons, all the way down to the far end, where the dance floor was already filling with shirtless guys. Steve was back with our drinks and another big smile. He was polite enough to try and include both of us in that smile, but he wasn't fooling me. Eric had already captured a piece of Steve's heart. I know, because Eric had that same effect on me. Once again, I marveled at how this guy could still be single at thirty.

"So, haven't seen you in here before," Steve said to Eric, ignoring a couple of customers signaling they needed drinks.

"I-I've never been here before," was Eric's reply.

"Do you plan on coming again?"

"Uh..."

"Yes, he plans on coming here a lot, don't you, Eric?" Steve shot me an annoyed look. Yeah, maybe I was pushing a bit strong.

"Be right back," Steve said, rushing off to his by now irate customers.

"He likes you," I told Eric. "You want me to disappear for a few minutes?"

"No!" An expression of near panic crossed his face.

"Just so you can get better acquainted."

"No!" He grabbed my arm. "Just don't say anything to annoy him."

I chuckled. "You caught that look, did you?"

"It was hard to miss. I can answer for myself, Jason, though I appreciate you being here with me."

"Are you feeling more relaxed?"

"Not the word I'd use, but not quite as nervous."

"That's good."

Steve was back. "Hey, I have a fifteen-minute break in a few. Wanna grab a table so we can talk a little more?" He made it sound as if I was included in the deal, so I nodded and looked around. There was a table way in the corner.

"We'll be over there," I said, taking Eric's arm and leading him away from the bar. My cell chimed at that moment. A text from Pete.

Hey, wanna meet at Bobby's Tavern?

I texted back. *I'm here already. Where are you?*

On my way. I'll see you in a few.

"That was my friend, Pete. He's on his way here so you'll get to meet him. He's really nice." He looked nervous again, so I added, "You'll like him." We reached the table and sat waiting for Steve. He arrived a couple of minutes later and sat next to Eric.

"Matt not on duty today?" I asked him by way of starting the conversation.

"No, he called out, said he was sick, so I'm pulling double shift. Just my luck when the most beautiful guy I've ever seen walks in. Normally I'd be off at six and could've asked you to stick around, Eric."

Eric looked appropriately taken aback by Steve's forward approach. I'd guess he'd never had anyone come on to him like that, man or woman. He seemed to recover pretty quick though.

"Wow, you don't waste any time, do you?"

"Not when this place is filled with a hundred guys all wanting to be where I am right now." Steve grinned at Eric. "Look around. I can feel the hate laser generated and pointed right between my eyes."

Eric laughed. "You're a riot. Are all bartenders equipped with that kind of dazzling repartee?"

I couldn't tell if Eric was being sarcastic or just amused, but Steve didn't seem to mind either way. "Yep, it's a must on the résumé—can talk the hind leg off a donkey."

"What do you do with the hind leg when you've talked it off?" Eric asked, deadpan, and the two of them laughed together.

I was most definitely feeling like the third wheel and was really happy to see Pete heading our way. I introduced him to Eric. Steve he knew already, it seemed. I got up and picked up my half-full glass. "Let me buy you a drink, Pete." I smiled at the new friends. "Be back shortly."

Eric didn't look too panicked, so I put my arm around Pete's shoulders and marched him over to the bar.

"So, how d'you know Eric?" Pete asked.

"He's the nephew of some friends of my folks," I replied, crossing my fingers against the white lie I'd just told. "He just recently came out so I said I'd take him to a couple of bars. He's kinda shy, but really nice."

"And you left him alone with Steve?"

"Is that bad? They hit it off right away and Eric needs to meet some guys. What'll you have?" Steve's relief bartender was hovering in front of us.

"Just a Bud Lite." Pete looked back to where Steve and Eric sat in deep conversation. "Steve's okay, but from what I hear he's not a relationship kind of guy."

"That's okay. They only met twenty minutes ago. I don't expect to hear wedding bells ringing, just yet. Like I said, Eric needs to meet guys, play the field, enjoy himself, *find* himself."

"He's certainly a good-looking dude. He looks tall."

"Wait till he stands up. He's six-five if he's an inch."

We shot the breeze for a while and I kept my eye on where Steve and Eric were sitting. When Steve got up to go back to work, he bent and kissed Eric on the cheek. Okay, nothing wrong with that and Eric seemed to enjoy it, even though he was blushing like mad. I steered Pete back to the table.

"So, did he ask you out? Pardon my pushiness."

Eric chuckled. "Yes, Tuesday night. We're going to a movie at Liberty Station."

"Great! You like him then."

"He's nice. Did you know he's studying for his environmental engineering degree?"

"No, but I didn't know him till the exact same time as you. Did you know, Pete?"

"Nope."

"What do you do, Pete?" Eric asked.

"I'm a teacher at Mosspointe High."

"Really? I bet the students love having such a handsome teacher."

Well, knock me sideways. Is Eric actually flirting with Pete?

"And you?" Pete leaned forward toward Eric. "Are you a model or an actor?"

Eric grinned. "Thanks, but I'm a financial advisor. Pretty boring most of the time, but it pays the bills."

"Wow, I thought you'd be right at home on a fashion runway or something."

Okay, maybe I should just leave and let them get on with their flirtiness, but somewhere in the conversation and only one extra drink later, I noticed Eric getting restless and I asked if he'd like to go someplace else.

"No, I think I'll head home, if you don't mind, but this has been great. Thanks, Jason, and nice meeting you, Pete."

I didn't argue the point. Some guys don't like noisy bars, and around five-thirty on a Sunday, the volume in Bobby's Tavern can get so that conversation is nearly impossible. Eric hugged Pete then me and kissed my cheek and whispered, "Call me this week," then left with a wave to Steve whose gaze followed him all the way to the door.

* * * *

I was surprised when Noah called me early the following morning as I was getting ready for work. "Hey, how are you, Jason?"

"I'm okay." I deliberately kept any warmth out of my reply.

"You still mad at me?"

"No, not mad, maybe a little irritated."

"I apologize if I sounded like I was lecturing you the other day. I just wanted to make sure you don't fall into the same kind of trap I did when I was new to this."

That sounded sincere enough. "I appreciate your concern, Noah. I think I was just pissed that you thought I couldn't handle the situation. That I'd let it get out of control. Eric is a sweetheart, but he knows our boundaries."

"Good. So, did you take him to the bar?"

"Yeah, and he had a great time. It was nice to see him relax into something he'd been scared to death of doing by himself. I think he might just enjoy getting out and meeting more people like himself."

I figured I'd leave out the part about his date with Steve. I'd wait to see what came of it. Chances were Eric would tell his uncle at some point and that would be fine.

"Did he ask if he could see you again?"

"He asked if I'd call him during the week, so I guess I will."

"You should. He's a good client to keep in touch with."

A twinge of irritation prickled on the back of my neck. Noah was right, but I still hated to think of Eric as a client. But he was, wasn't he? He knew that if we had sex again, it would be as a paying customer. Those were the parameters of our relationship and he'd said he was okay with it. So why wasn't I? It wasn't as if I foresaw any kind of romance between us, but I liked Eric and thought he'd be a good friend. I knew it would definitely annoy Noah if I mentioned anything remotely like that.

"You still there, Jason?"

"Oh yeah, sorry. I was just thinking about what you said, and you're right of course. How are things your end?"

"Good. Busy weekend. I met a new client and he's keen to become a regular."

I groaned inwardly. Noah and I were never going to be more than occasional friends. Time to accept it and put any thoughts of other possibilities firmly on the back-burner, if not off the stove all together.

"That's good," I said, trying to sound enthusiastic, but God, it was hard.

"Okay, Jason, just wanted to make sure we were still friends."

"Of course we are. Am I going to see you anytime soon?"

"If you're up in Sherman Oaks, maybe, visiting your parents. San Diego's a bit too far for me right now."

Right, what with your full schedule…

We said our goodbyes shortly after that. Depression was the name of the game as I finished dressing, left the apartment and headed downtown to the office. Even Hank's over-the-top tales of his weekend in Paradise, also known as Lewis, couldn't quite shake me out of it. I smiled often enough though just to let him know I was listening. I really was happy for Hank. He totally deserved to find someone like Lewis who from all accounts, or at least Hank's, was the sweetest, kindest man in all the world, and without equal in bed.

Phil without John joined us at the coffee machine and actually managed a gruff 'good morning' as he poured himself a cup. I replied in kind and asked him how he'd enjoyed his weekend.

"It was okay. The wife took off to visit her sister in Alhambra so me and the kids went to the movies."

"What did you see?" Hank asked.

"Some dumb thing about a dragon. The kids liked it, though. How about you guys?"

Wow, an extended conversation from Phil. Is this some kind of breakthrough?

"I was with my boyfriend," Hank said. "We didn't have time for a movie."

Saucy.

Phil blinked. He'd got the inference all right. "That's, uh…great."

"I took a friend of mine's nephew to a gay bar," I told him. "His first time ever."

"Oh yeah? How'd it go?"

"Well, he's six-five, and a blond Adonis, so how'd you think it went?"

To my surprise—and Hank's, I'm sure—Phil chuckled. "Even I can figure that one out."

Any further camaraderie was stifled when John came around the corner, frowning no doubt at the sight of the three of us with actual smiles on our faces.

"What's going on?" he asked Phil.

"Oh, just shooting the breeze about our weekends," Phil replied. John stared at him as if he'd lost his mind, but said nothing, just grunted and walked away.

Phil rolled his eyes. "Nice talking to you," he said and sauntered over to his desk.

Hank and I exchanged what-the-fuck expressions and went to work on yet another project William had set up for us.

"You know, Hank…" I glanced into William's office to make sure he was there. "You and I should start up our own software biz. We work so well together. What d'you think?"

"Don't even think about it," William yelled from behind his desk.

I laughed and blew him a kiss, which he pretended to bat away from him. Another fun day at Sonar Electronics.

Chapter Fourteen

Tuesday, there was an envelope among the usual junk mail and flyers sure to be found in my mailbox, when I got home. A letter from Simon, thanking me for taking care of his nephew. Apparently Eric had called him with all good things to say about me. Sweet guy.

I am enclosing your check, Jason, and I have added a small bonus along with my thanks, Your friend, Simon Foster.

The small bonus was an extra five hundred dollars. I whistled through my teeth as I read that part. Simon really was *da bomb* as they say...or at least I think that's what they say.

Which reminded me that this was the night for Eric's date with Steve and I wondered how that was going to pan out. Steve was handsome without a doubt and a good personality to go with the looks. I just hoped he didn't try to rush Eric straight into bed, which, coming from me, I guess was a bit ironical, if not hypocritical.

But what Eric and I did was different, I told myself. He came to me knowing what to expect.

With Steve, it would be a different kind of connection. More emotional. Eric might be hoping he'd met *the one*, while Steve who, of course, was far more experienced, could possibly be regarding this as simply getting some more tail. I hoped not, but hey, there wasn't much I could do about it, now was there? I had a feeling I'd be getting a call from Eric quite soon.

I called Matt to see how he was doing and listened to his sneezing and coughing for as long as I could stand it before wishing him well and hanging up. So, home alone on a Tuesday night and happy to have some down time from all the excitement of the last few days. Microwaved pizza, a beer and Netflix, the perfect combination.

My cell rang just as I was about to turn in. A text from Eric.

Thanks for being pushy on Sunday at the bar. Steve is fantastic. Seeing him again on his next night off. Smiley face Smiley face I'll call you tomorrow. I need a favor. XOX

Well, isn't that great? I wonder what the favor is?

* * * *

I have to admit to being more than a tad curious as to what Eric's 'favor' was so instead of waiting for his call, I called him when I got home Wednesday night. I hadn't forgotten that David, the guy I met in the gym, wanted to hook up on Thursday when he was back in town. I hoped Eric didn't want to plan something for that night also. I really didn't want to ask David for another raincheck, plus I was quite keen on seeing him again. Something in that brief meeting at the gym had stirred a definite interest in me.

Eric sounded pleased to hear from me. "Can I come over? I have your fee…"

"Forget that," I almost snapped, already embarrassed. "Just come over and tell me what's on your mind."

"Okay, be there in about fifteen minutes."

I tidied up the place a bit while I waited then took a quick shower and slipped on a pair of shorts and a T-shirt. He was prompt like the first time but seemed excited rather than nervous. He looked great as always and he initiated the hug and kiss.

"You're glowing," I told him, stepping back from his embrace. I walked into the kitchen to get us a couple of beers.

"I hope I'm not reading too much into my date with Steve last night, but he seemed to really like me," he said, accepting the can of beer I thrust at him.

"That's an easy thing to do, Eric. You're very likeable. My friend Pete liked you too."

I watched his expression as he tried to remember who Pete was. "Oh, yeah, he was cute."

Chuckling, I said, "Yeah, it was all about Steve on Sunday."

"He's so nice, Jason, and he kisses almost as good as you."

I choked on my beer. "*Almost?* Don't ever tell him that."

"Well, you were the first guy I ever kissed so there's bound to be a comparison, and you have the edge…just."

"Eric, you haven't told Steve about how we met, I hope."

"Oh no, that will remain our little secret."

Thank fuck for that. The last thing I needed to get broadcast was what I did occasionally on the side.

"Okay, come sit and tell me what's on your mind."

He followed me over to the couch and sat with one long leg tucked under him, facing me. "So, last night after the movie, we went for a snack and we talked a lot. He's really interesting, a bit of a rough childhood, but he didn't dwell on it. I figured we could talk more of that another time. He drove me home and we made out in the car for a while, then he asked if he could come up to my place, and I said no. Well, not as abruptly as that, but I got cold feet, Jason. He seemed okay with it, but I could tell he wanted more from me, and I…wasn't ready. Stupid, huh?"

"No, not stupid," I told him. "It has to feel right for you."

"Yeah, but I'm thirty years old, Jason. I don't get to act like some silly debutante. I read somewhere that thirty in gay years is *old*, really old, so when a handsome, younger-than-me dude like Steve wants to put the make on me, I should go for it, right?"

I held back my urge to laugh. I didn't think he'd appreciate it at that moment. He just looked so damned adorable in all his earnestness.

"I want to give you a blow job," he said.

I almost choked on my beer again. "What?"

"I want you to tell me if I'm any good at it. I know eventually Steve and I are going to get to that point, and you, of all people, should be able to tell me if I'm any good at it, or not."

"Why me of all people?"

"Because of your, you know, profession."

"Oh." I swear I could feel the backs of my ears burning. "Right." I guess the wrong answer here would be *I'm no expert.*

"So, can I?" He gave me that earnest expression again. "I have your fee right here."

"Eric, I am not going to charge you for giving me a blow job. I should be paying you!"

He laughed. "You're funny." He leaned in and kissed me. "And so sexy."

Okay, so call me easy, or slut, or whatever, but who the hell could resist an offer like this from such an amazing-looking guy? I spread my legs and he immediately got between them and unfastened my shorts. I lifted my hips so he could slide the shorts down. I wasn't wearing briefs so it was easy access for him. Of course, I was hard. A kiss from Eric and just the sight of his beautiful face about to dive into my groin were enough.

He gripped my cock at the base then licked the tip. I moaned out encouragement and ran my fingers through his thick blond hair as he swirled his remarkably long tongue around the head before dipping in to chase the pre-cum bubbling up from the slit. He looked up at me, searching for approval, I guess, and I gave it to him without any hesitation.

"That is so good, Eric," I managed to gasp. This guy didn't need any pointers from me, but who was I to stop him now that we were both so into it? If Steve showed half the enthusiasm I was exhibiting, he'd make Eric feel like a champ. He sucked me in all the way, his tongue working overtime on both the up and the down strokes and he was bringing me to the edge at an alarming rate.

"Okay, stop for a moment," I said, easing out of his mouth. "Some guys are really into ball play too, so while you're blowing him, you can caress his balls, slide a finger over his taint…you know what that is, right?" He nodded. "Then maybe finger his hole, see if he responds to that."

So the 'lesson' continued and Eric came through with flying colors. "You're a natural at this," I told him, panting heavily. I was going to come and didn't know if he'd want it in his mouth again. Better to warn him. "Eric, I'm so close." He mumbled something but didn't stop and before I could pull out I was hit with another doozy of an orgasm and he was humming and choking and swallowing and gripping my thighs so hard I was going to be sporting a few bruises when he was done.

"Fuck, Eric…that was amazing. You are more than ready for the real thing with Steve."

"That was pretty real," he said, wiping his mouth with the back of his hand.

"It was. Come up here." I pretended to hoist his big frame over me, but he did all the work, straddling my chest, his erection leaking pre-cum over my shirt. I lowered my head and took his cock between my lips. He must have been working on it while he sucked me because he came before I really had time to get more than a few licks in. He tasted so good, I didn't mind and let him stay there with my nose pressed into his pubes. He smelled good too.

When he rolled off me, we lay back on the couch, breathing heavily, our legs tangled together, our clothes a mess of sweat and semen. I huffed out a laugh. "If our friends could see us now." He laughed too then tickled me. I lay on top of him and we shared some hot, deep kisses. We snuggled and dozed and when I came to, the room was in darkness.

Wow, must have had quite the snooze. He woke and stared blearily at me. "Wanna shower before you leave?" I asked. "I'd ask you to stay but I have an early call in the morning."

"Shit, me too. I didn't mean to fall asleep." He got off the couch. "I'll shower when I get home." He kissed me gently. "Thank you, Jason...for everything." We kissed again then he murmured, "Goodbye," and headed for the door.

I saw him out then got ready for bed. The goodbye he'd uttered bothered me. Had he realized that any ongoing 'business' relationship with me would not sit well with a future boyfriend? Be it Steve or some other lucky stiff. Had he decided to cut ties with me? And when I thought about it, why would he need to continue seeing me if he had a steady boyfriend? I was pretty certain that Steve could keep him happy in a long-term relationship. Anyway, I wished him the best. He was a sweet, sweet, guy and if asking me to judge his blow job skills had been a ruse just to see one last time, I was okay with that.

It wasn't until morning when I went into the kitchen to make my coffee that I saw he'd left four one hundred bills under the coffee can. I had no idea when he'd have had the time to do that. Well, I guess he'd wanted to keep our relationship on the right track.

Noah would be pleased.

I got a call from David at lunchtime asking if I was free to have dinner with him. I said yes, determined to have what might pass for a regular date without banking on some hot and heavy sex to round the evening out. I know I'd laughed at that idea before, but maybe I craved a touch of normality in my life. It had been anything but, for the last few weeks, and David seemed like the kind of guy who'd be okay with taking things slow. What I based that assumption on, I have no idea. Just a feeling, I guess.

David had said he'd pick me up at seven, so when I got home after work, I took a long shower then surveyed my closet for something nice to wear on this first date with him. And when I thought about it, this was my first real date since Darren had left me. I couldn't even regard my dinner with Noah as a date. Since then I'd always had the idea that it had been simply a ways and means of getting me involved in his male escort business. I still liked Noah, but I knew there was no future for him and me, so why waste my time pining over someone who had a very different view of what the future held for him?

I eventually chose a pale blue polo shirt and beige pants to wear. California casual which is acceptable in all but the most highfalutin' restaurants in town. The doorbell rang at seven. Another prompt guy. I swung the door open and was rewarded by David's smile and the fact that he looked even better than I remembered.

"Hi, come on in."

He stepped inside and I, forward hussy that I am, wrapped him up in a big hug.

"Hi," he said on a chuckle. "This is the kind of greeting I like."

"Good." I kissed his cheek. Not on the lips yet. "Would you like a pre-dinner drink or are we heading out right away?"

"We have time for a quick one."

I burst out laughing and after a second he joined in. "If I'd meant that as a come-on, I'd be ashamed of myself for its cheesiness."

"I like you already," I said. "So, there's Scotch, vodka or beer for your delight."

He grinned. "A short Scotch on the rocks, please." He stood by the kitchen counter as I made our drinks. "You look nice. That shirt goes great with your eyes."

"Thank you, kind sir, and while we're on the subject, you look pretty darned good too." As I handed him his glass, I took a moment to drink in his hazel eyes and lush mouth. I fingered the collar of his green shirt. "Perfect color for you…"

He surprised me by lowering his head and kissing the back of my hand as it lingered on his collar. Our eyes met and he smiled and the air between us seemed to be charged with electricity. The only other time I had experienced such a palpable rush of attraction was the first time I'd met Darren—and why did I keep thinking of him every time I met someone new?

"Well, here's to you and me, and a beautiful night together." He raised his glass to mine, his voice low and husky and, to my ears, filled with a sexy promise of things to come. And come I would if he used that voice in my ear while we lay in bed together…

Oh my God, pull yourself together. The guy's been here barely ten minutes and you're imagining him fucking you!

"Yes…" My reply was more than just a tad shaky. "To you and me." We clinked glasses and I threw back most of my Scotch, hoping it would steady my nerves. I was behaving like Hector the time he'd been alone with me in his hotel room.

"Okay?" He was looking at me with concern. "You seem nervous."

"No, just...hungry." It was the only thing I could think of to account for my shaking hand.

"Oh, of course, it's been a long day for you, I'm sure." He set his glass down on the counter. "Let's go then. I hope you like French cooking."

"Love it," I said, taking his hand and leading him to the door. Right then I just wanted to get out of the apartment before I did or said something stupid and spoiled our evening before it started.

He'd chosen a local restaurant, so the drive was short. I'd been to La Grande Bouche once before and had enjoyed it, especially their wine selection. On the way over we'd chatted about mundane things like the convention he'd just attended and my job, but it was nice, not boring. The restaurant was set up like a Paris bistro. Small tables and cane-back chairs, lots of plants, and mellow jazz softly playing in the background. My kind of place...and my kind of dinner companion. David was charming. Warm, intelligent, humorous and, not to forget, hot. Everything I needed and wanted in a boyfriend.

"So, are you a San Diego native, Jason?" he asked.

"No, California native, though. I was raised in Sherman Oaks. My parents still live there. And you're from Sacramento?"

"Yes."

"Your folks still there?"

"My father is. My mother died some years ago."

"Oh, I'm sorry. How's your dad?"

"I'm afraid my father and I aren't on the best of terms. He didn't take the news that I'm gay very well. Even though I came out to him, and my mother, when I was still in high school, he's never come to terms with it. My mother accepted it, and my sister, Adele… She and I are best friends, really."

"Is she married"

"Yes, to a sweet woman, Rosalyn. They have two children."

"Wow! How did your dad take that?"

"Not well, but the children worked their magic on him. He's been to their home a few times. The kids like him."

There was a momentary flicker of sadness in his expression and I wanted to reach across the table and hold his hand, but at that moment the waiter arrived to take our drink order. David ordered a bottle of Pinot Noir after asking if I liked wine.

"I'll just have a glass if you'd rather have a Scotch."

"No, wine's good," I told him. "I'll enjoy sharing it with you."

"You have a lovely smile, Jason," he said after the waiter left. "With just a hint of tease in it."

"Me, tease?" I affected mock horror and he laughed.

"I think you know very well you do, and how it affects people around you. It's part of your charm."

I grinned. "You know all the right things to say."

"Only when I mean them."

"Thanks for sharing about your family. I'm glad you and your sister are such good friends."

He nodded. "She's the best. You have siblings?"

"Nope, the only child. The original spoiled brat." I chuckled. "Not really, but my parents have always been supportive of me, even when I sometimes didn't make the right choices."

"That's wonderful to hear. I always said if I ever had kids I'd love them no matter what."

"You want kids?"

"Well, I'm thirty-four, and the chances of me marrying a woman are pretty remote, so probably won't happen."

"You can adopt," I pointed out.

"True. How about you, Jason? You like kids?"

I couldn't believe we were taking about having a family on our first date. It should've been scary, but I didn't see any sign of a deranged madman in his gentle smile.

"Yeah, I like them well enough, but you know, wrong kind of plumbing."

He laughed. A deep melodious sound. "You can adopt."

"Touché."

Our wine arrived and David engaged the waiter in polite conversation as he fussed over the glasses and the wine pouring. Hopefully, the subject of children-making was over. When the waiter left, we toasted each other and, as I gazed across at David, I had a mad moment when I envisioned lots of nights like this, he and I, sharing a meal, fine wine and, afterward, sharing a bed and making love into the wee small hours.

"Where are you?" he asked, his lush lips curled at the corners in a questioning smile.

"Right here, with you," I replied, my face a little warm at being caught daydreaming.

Our time together that night just seemed to speed away, over so soon, and oh, I didn't want to say goodnight and let him go. Sitting in his Range Rover Evoque outside my apartment building after he'd driven me home felt like one of the most awkward moments of my life. I wanted to ask him to come upstairs with me, and for probably the first time ever, I was tongue-tied. I just didn't want him to say 'How about a raincheck?' or worse, an outright 'Thanks, but no thanks'.

In the middle of my awkwardness, he leaned across from his seat and lightly kissed my cheek. Then, with his hand on my chin he turned my face toward him, and laid a much firmer kiss on my mouth. His lips were warm and soft on mine and what could I do but open to him? He didn't deepen the kiss though, just whispered, "I had an amazing time tonight, Jason. I hope we can do it again, soon."

His warm breath was intoxicating and my lips tingled with desire under his. "Yes, please," I whispered back. "Really soon."

"I'll call you tomorrow."

Okay, that was plain enough. Get out of the car, Jason.

I stood on the sidewalk watching until his Evoque disappeared around the corner. My shoulders slumped and I called myself all the dopes in the world for not asking him in. Even if he'd said no, he'd have known I was *interested*. My cell rang as I trudged my way upstairs to my apartment. I glanced at the caller screen. Matt. I'd call him tomorrow. Once inside I poured myself a stiff drink, undressed and pulled on a pair of boxer shorts. I sat on the couch nursing my drink and wondering why I was depressed. I'd had a great evening with a super guy that I definitely wanted to see again.

Get over yourself, dummy. You told yourself you wanted a normal date, with a goodnight kiss and a promise of another date, and that's what you got. So be sensible and see it for what it is.

Yeah, next date I'm asking him in without a moment's hesitation.

Chapter Fifteen

I didn't check for messages until the following morning. There were two. One from Hector and one from Russ. I didn't even know he had my number. Hector was asking for another appointment. Same hotel, same night, in a week's time. Russ was going to be in San Diego. He had a friend he was hooking up with and wanted to know if I would join them. I wondered if Noah knew about his clients making arrangements on their own. No way was I going to agree to Russ's request without letting Noah aware of what was being asked of me.

At the same time, I wasn't sure if I wanted to continue in the escort business. Yes, it could be lucrative, and so far hadn't taken up too much of my time. Evenings and weekends were easy to arrange. But my night out with David had given me a different perspective on my life. Was I really going to be content ambling through the future, dating here and there, and giving happiness at a price to insecure guys? If I wanted to have a shot at a relationship with David, I couldn't in all honesty be sleeping with other men, regardless of the fact there was no emotional entanglement on my side.

If David found out I had paying customers, I couldn't imagine he'd be thrilled about it. I didn't know David that well yet, but in the time we'd shared I got the impression he was one of those 'stand-up' kind of guys. True blue, loyal, steadfast—that sort of thing—and just the kind of man I wanted in my life. Someone who'd bring me stability. That might have sounded kind of boring, but I suspected that word wouldn't apply to David.

My cell rang. *Speak, or rather think of the devil...* "Hi, David, how are you?"

"If my answer was, missing you, would that seem too pushy?"

I chuckled. "Push away. I like being missed by you."

"Are you free tonight?"

"Well, there might be a small charge." Oops, maybe that wasn't the best answer, considering what I'd been up to.

He laughed. "Whatever it is, I'll be happy to pay. I was wondering if you'd like to come over to my place, have a drink, something to eat...I'm not a bad cook."

"That sounds fantastic. Thank you, I'd love to come over."

"Great. Here's my address..." He reeled it off. "Say about seven?"

"Perfect. What can I bring?"

"Just you and that beautiful smile of yours."

I chuckled. "Flattery will get you anything you want."

"Good to know. Okay, see you at seven. I have to run. I'm already late for a meeting."

"Bye, David." I set my cell aside and felt a sudden surge of excitement. I had a notion this would be a very good date.

Hank was in seventh heaven when I saw him at the office later. This was the weekend Lewis had asked him to go to Palm Springs and Hank was straining at the bit, trying to wish the day away so he and Lewis could get it on.

"What are *your* plans?" he managed to ask after almost giving me a blow-by-blow itinerary of what Lewis had arranged for them.

"I have a date tonight," I told him, trying to keep the smugness out of my voice.

"Oh, with Matt?"

"No, with David."

"Who?"

Oh right, I hadn't mentioned meeting David at the gym or our dinner plans for the previous night. "Sorry, David Farmer. He's a guy I met in the gym a couple of weeks ago. We had dinner last night and he wants to see me again tonight."

"Nice." Hank gave me what he considered a *knowing* look. "So, is this serious?"

"Hardly. I met him at the gym, I saw him last night for dinner and tonight I'm going to his apartment for drinks and something to eat. Not enough time to get serious, Hank."

"Hmm. Invited to his place, huh? *He* might be thinking in serious terms."

"Well, that's fine. It's time I got over Darren, and David might just be the one to help me do it."

"Well, I wish you the best." Hank squeezed my arm. "And I agree about the Darren jerk. All he deserves is to be someone that you used to love."

"Couldn't have put it better myself."

A shadow fell over the coffee cups then someone pushed me aside. "What are you girls gossiping about now?"

I whirled around to see John's pugnacious face screwed up into what he presumed was machoism. "I beg your fucking pardon, shithead?" I folded my arms and blocked his way to the coffee.

"You heard," he muttered. "William's not here today to save your swishing asses, so get out of my way." He pushed me again and I hauled off and socked him one.

He screamed blue murder, clutching his nose and staggering away from me. Phil and a couple of other employees came to see what was going on.

"He fucking broke my nose!" John yelled.

"And you deserved it," Hank hissed at him.

Phil's expression was one of total surprise as he stared at me. "What happened?"

"He started in with his homophobic bullshit, pushed me twice, so I hit him." I glared at Phil. "And I'll do it again if he doesn't cut it out. Just because William has a day off does not mean he can run rampant in here, being the asshole bully he is."

"I'm gonna see you fired," John shrieked at me in a very unmanly manner.

"I doubt it," I told him. "William's been adamant about the zero-tolerance policy of this company, but you chose to ignore it and insult your colleagues. Well, I for one am not having it anymore. You can take your complaints to Human Resources, but they'll find you in the wrong, John, and you know it."

"Fucking faggot!"

"John…" Phil tugged on his arm. "Go back to your desk and shut up. Jason's right. You are being stupid now and you need to calm down."

"You're taking his side?" John gaped at his office buddy.

"Honestly? I can't believe that you would go out of your way to make trouble here after what William said. Sorry, man, but I'm not putting my job on the line for you. Keep this up and William will fire your ass." Phil turned to the other employees. "I don't think I'm alone is this either, right?"

"Traitor," John mumbled and lurched away, heading for the restroom.

"Well…" Wendy, who sat at the desk next to mine, grinned at me. "You certainly know how to liven up the place. And I agree with you, Phil. John is a troublemaker, always has been."

Turned out John's nose wasn't broken, just bloody and puffy. I knew he was going to hate me forever, but the lack of support from everyone else, especially Phil, left him deflated and morose, probably concocting all kinds of scenarios in which I died a horrible death. Maybe now that he knew gay guys could actually punch, he'd simmer down. If not, it would be HR for the two of us.

At lunch, Hank was still a bit bug-eyed with how I'd handled John. "I couldn't believe it when you punched him," he gushed. "Wait till I tell Lewis!"

"And you can tell him you had my back through it all," I said. "He'll most likely give you even more lovin' in Palm Springs."

"Oh, I cannot wait."

"I just bet you can't."

Later, I wondered how William would react when he got the story, as he surely would. I knew he'd be pissed with John after his zero-tolerance speech, but he wouldn't be thrilled with me punching the idiot. *Oh, well, what's done is done,* I mused on the way home, and I had better things to think about, starting with my date with David.

My cell rang the minute I got in the apartment. *Matt. Shit.* I hadn't called him back.

"Hi, Matt."

"You didn't return my call."

"Yeah, sorry. Are you feeling better?"

"Totally better. Wanna get together tonight?"

"Can't tonight, Matt. I have a date."

"A *date*? Who with?"

Whoa, kinda belligerent. "A guy I met. We've been talking on the phone for a week or so, and we had dinner last night."

"And he wants to see you again *tonight*?"

"You make it sound as if that were impossible," I told him testily. "I am quite sought after, you know." I hoped he recognized humor when he heard it.

"Yeah, sorry, didn't mean to be snarky. Well, shit, what am I gonna do? This is my last day of sick leave. I'm back to work tomorrow and I can't switch with Steve. He says he has a big date. Shit, everybody's got dates except me."

"Don't worry, your turn will come. Not many guys can resist your pretty face and big guns."

"Huh. You're resisting them."

"Matt, go out. You won't be on your own very long."

"True. Okay, have fun tonight on your *date*."

Let it go, Matt. So Steve had a big date tomorrow night. *Who could that be with, I wonder?* I smiled at the thought of Eric's excitement. I knew I shouldn't, but I would want to call him Sunday to see how it went. Well, I hoped. Really well.

I showered then changed into the softest pair of jeans I had that hugged my crotch and ass just right. I added my favorite Perry Ellis polo shirt. It had been laundered so many times the original color had faded to a pale creamy beige. Somehow it always looked and felt good on me. On my way over to David's, I stopped at the liquor store and bought a bottle of Pinot Noir. I remembered that was what he'd ordered at our dinner last night.

His apartment building in Mission Hills was easy to find. High-end behind a security gate and I noticed a couple of cameras screening the walkway from the guest parking to the main entrance. He buzzed me in and I rode the elevator to the fourth floor. He was there on the landing when I got off and greeted me with a big smile and a hug. He smelled nice and looked even better in a short-sleeve checkered shirt untucked over white shorts. It was good to be held in his muscled arms so I prolonged the hug and nestled my face in the crook of his neck.

"Good to see you," he murmured against my cheek, his warm lips sending chills down my spine. He led me to his apartment door and once inside I handed him the bottle of wine. "Oh, a favorite of mine. I have Scotch if you'd like one."

"Thanks, just a light one as I'm driving."

He nodded. "Very responsible of you."

I chuckled. "That's me all right." I looked around his place and could tell he hadn't lived here very long. Furnishings were a bit sparse, but he seemed to have all the kitchen essentials.

"I'm in the process of buying a condo, hence the minimalist look," he said, as if he'd caught what I was thinking. "This place came furnished. Not exactly my style, but it's only for another month or two till the escrow closes."

"Nice. Will you be in the same area?"

"Yeah, next street over." He handed me my drink. "Cheers." He touched his wineglass to mine.

"Cheers. If you need any help moving, I'll volunteer."

"Thanks. I'll definitely remember that. So how was your day?"

I laughed. "You might not believe this, but I punched one of my fellow workers on the nose this morning."

"What? What the hell happened?"

"He's a homophobic asshole who has already been told to cool it by the boss and reminded of the company's zero-tolerance policy. But he chose to ignore it because William, our boss, was out of the office and he thought he could play the bully."

"And you got into a fight?"

"Well, it was too short to call a fight. He called me and Hank—he's another gay guy in the office—*girls*, then he shoved me, twice, so I punched him. I wasn't exactly aiming for his nose, but it got in the way, I guess."

"Oh, my God, Jason."

"I know, I couldn't believe I'd done it, afterward. Fortunately, the rest of the staff supported me, 'cause I know when William finds out, if he hasn't already, he's not going to be happy with me."

"He won't fire you, will he?"

"No, I don't think so, just a reprimand. Of course, HR will hear about it, so there will be repercussions of some kind. William and I are actually pretty friendly. He was there for me when—well, never mind about that. One drama a day is enough for you to hear about."

"But I want to hear everything about you."

Not everything. "Another time. I'll tell you all about my dark and mysterious past when I know you better."

"Which is what I intend you do." He gave me what was almost a shy smile that made him seem years younger. "I'm really glad you could make it tonight. I enjoyed our first date very much."

"Me too," I said, glad that we'd veered away from a subject I wasn't ready to enlarge upon at that moment. I had other things in mind for David and myself. "I loved that you wanted to get together again so soon."

"It wasn't *too* soon? To be honest, I wondered if you'd think I was being a bit overly eager."

"What does overly eager feel like?" I asked with a teasing smile.

"Uh, I guess it's what I'm feeling right now."

"Well, if it helps, I like you overly eager." I took a step closer to him and laid a light kiss on his lips. "It's very flattering, and I told you that would get you anything you want."

He put an arm around my waist and held me while he pressed his lips more firmly to mine. I opened for him and his tongue gliding over mine sent a thrill straight to my groin. "These glasses are in the way," I mumbled, and he took mine and set it down on the counter along with his.

He pulled me closer, both arms around me now, the kiss we shared growing in intensity. I'd kissed a lot of men in the past few weeks and foolishly had measured them all against Darren's, most of them coming up short, apart from maybe Noah's. But this…this was something else. Not that his technique was that much different. I mean a kiss is still a kiss, after all, some better, some not so hot, and yet, everything about David kissing me seemed just so right. He made me feel needed and wanted, and not just for sex, although, as far as I was concerned that was most definitely on the table. There was just something so meaningful in the way he caressed me, both with his hands and with his lips. It was as though I was under his spell, putty in his hands. I was literally shaking with desire and excitement, the earlier wretchedness of the day forgotten.

"Jason," he whispered on a breath into my mouth as I wound my arms around his neck and deepened our kiss. He slipped his hands under my shirt, tracing my spine with his fingertips, then, sinking his hands under the waistband of my jeans, he cupped my butt cheeks and pulled me in even closer, pressing his very obvious erection against mine.

"Mmm…" I ground my crotch over his and he groaned, obviously enjoying the frottage. I slid my hands down his back and palmed his muscular ass to hold him in place as we writhed together. This was my idea of heaven. Holding and being held by this marvelous man, drowning in desire and so ready to give him everything and anything he wanted. Hard as it was to tear my mouth away from David's, I wanted to explore more of him. His shirt was open just enough for me to get my lips on his left nipple and I wasted no time in teasing and nibbling on the already hard nub. He shuddered against me. *Good, he likes nipple play…*

I unbuttoned the rest of his shirt and ran my hands over his hard torso. His skin was smooth with just a light dusting of sandy-colored hair across his chest. He was tugging at the hem of my polo, so I raised my arms to let him slip it over my head. Our bare chests slapped together, always an exciting part of making out for me. I've always loved that first slide of warm skin on skin. It feels like a promise of even better sensations to come. I had a momentary twinge of 'are we going too fast?', but I couldn't have stopped what was happening even if a herd of elephants had come crashing through the door.

What I wanted was him naked and on his bed and was just about to say so, when he took my hand and led me into the bedroom. Great minds and all that. We finished undressing each other then I stepped back just a little so that I could see all of him. Just as I had imagined, he was stunning. His time at the gym had obviously paid off, but had not left him overly muscled, sleeker and more toned, and in my eyes, close to perfection. His cock was hard and glistening and begging for my attention.

"Like what you see?" he asked, grinning.

"You bet," I said, closing the gap between us. He took me in his arms and kissed my lips, my throat, my shoulders then my chest, teasing each nipple with his tongue and teeth until I thought I'd go mad with ecstasy.

He lifted his head to gaze into my eyes. "I like what I see, too, Jason. The moment I saw you at the gym that day, I wanted you. I want you even more now, every part of you." He dropped to his knees and took my already swollen cock into his mouth, swallowing me to the hilt. I gasped from the heat of his mouth and from the way he held me there while he swirled his tongue up and down my engorged length. Oh my God, he was good, too good, for as he sucked, a tingling sensation spread from the base of my spine into my balls, signaling that I was about to come. Was he ready for me or should I pull out? I uttered a warning sound and clutched at his short-cropped hair.

"David," I groaned. "I'm..."

He cupped my butt in his big hands and pulled me even farther into his mouth and I couldn't hold back another second. I moaned his name, clutching this time at his shoulders as my knees seemed to melt and my body shuddered in the throes of my orgasm. He held me steady until I came down from the high of my climax. Even then he continued to gently suck on my cock until the sensation overload became too much and I had to pull out.

He stood, running his hands up my arms till he framed my face and brushed my lips with his then wrapped his arms around me, holding me while I silently reveled in the strength of his embrace. He lowered me onto the bed and lay on his side over me, stroking my chest and laying gentle kisses on my face.

"I knew you would taste better than the wine I had earlier," he murmured. "Tangy, but sweet."

Gazing at his ruggedly handsome face, at his hazel eyes now an almost dark green from the soft lighting in the room, I counted myself as one lucky guy to be here with him. I reached up to stroke his face then tug him down so I could kiss him properly. The touch of his lips on mine, the sudden urgency of his kiss was enough to get me going again, but this time I wanted it to be all about him. I rolled him onto his back and straddled him, peppering his chest and abs with little nipping kisses and sensual licks that him writhing under me. With the tip of my tongue, I traced the treasure trail of sandy blond hair that started at his navel. His erection pushed into the crack of my ass and I imagined it sliding, bare, inside me. *Maybe, another time…* I scooted down to take it in my mouth, running my tongue over the swollen head, tasting him, inhaling his musky scent. David gasped and moaned, sounds that told me he was enjoying this as much as I was. His cock pulsed and throbbed in my mouth, spilling pre-cum onto my tongue. I sucked him in to the back of my throat and he groaned out loud.

"Wait," he whispered, and pulled out.

"Was I doing it wrong?" I asked, teasing, knowing full well that wasn't the reason.

"You're doing it all too well. I had in mind to fuck you, if you'll let me."

"Mmm… How can I deny someone who asks so nicely?"

He flipped me onto my back and knelt between my thighs then went down on me, licking and sucking my cock until I was fully hard again. He lifted my legs over his shoulders and continued driving me crazy by sucking on my balls before pushing his face into my ass crack. Wow. I hadn't expected this. I don't know why, but from the way David was circling my hole with the tip of his tongue, it was obvious he was no novice. I lifted my hips to give him more access and he fucked me slowly and deliberately with his tongue. I clutched at the sheet under me with both hands as the heat of his tongue invaded me and sent frissons of exquisite sensations rippling over my skin.

I gasped and cried out and writhed under him and told him he was the most amazing man in the whole fucking world and to please never stop what he was doing. Words that I remembered later and flushed with embarrassment, but at that moment I meant every fucking syllable. A finger joined his tongue, going deeper, caressing my prostate, adding even more sensation to my already over-heated body. I grabbed his shoulders almost in protest and suddenly his sexy, smiling face was hovering over me.

"Ready for me?"

"God yes," I managed to choke out and he leaned away to open his nightstand. He kissed me as he inserted his lubed fingers deep inside me, once more grazing my prostate and sending tiny sparks of pleasure through me. I watched as he sheathed his cock. It looked bigger and harder than before, and even more beautiful. I felt like gurgling with joy knowing that any second now it was going to be inside me, filling me up. Impatiently, I arched myself toward him as he guided his erection to my opening. I relished the initial burn when he entered me and thrust my ass onto his cock.

"Impatient much?" he murmured.

"Only for you," I muttered. "Wanna feel you deep inside me, David. Fuck me…"

"Yesss," David hissed through his teeth. "Love being inside you, Jason, so hot, so beautiful…"

I wrapped my arms around his neck and tugged him down for a long, loaded kiss that was wet and sloppy, all lips and tongues, and moans, mostly from me. I was never quiet in bed. David seemed to like it, burying himself deeper inside me and picking up the pace with long ramming thrusts that sent me into a state of near delirium. My cock, trapped between our bodies, was throbbing like mad and I was going to come at any moment. I tried hard to hold on while he fucked me like the champion I knew he'd be. I caressed his face, his back, the sides of his muscled torso, cupped his butt and pulled him in like I was trying for the deepest fuck of my life.

I yelled out his name when a torrent of hot cum coated both our chests, my breath stuttering from me as my orgasm overwhelmed me. He stiffened in my arms then shuddered. A long groan escaped his lips and he plunged inside me, once, twice before I felt the heat of his cum through the condom's thin latex. He collapsed over me but fell on his side, dragging me into his arms, holding me in a tight embrace and kissing me as if I were the last human on earth.

"My God," I whispered when we came up for air, "you are amazing. I don't think I've ever been so thoroughly fucked in my life…in the best possible way, of course." I wriggled my ass over his cock, still tight inside me. "I bet you'd be hard again in a few minutes."

He kissed my nose. "Does the word 'insatiable' mean anything to you?"

"Yeah, but like Oliver Twist, I'd like some more, sir," I said, making him laugh.

"After we eat and shower…maybe shower first. We're kinda glued together…" He slipped out of me and I whined, making him laugh again. "You are a baby. Come on, let's take a quick shower together."

That got my immediate interest. Anywhere I could press my nakedness to his was fine with me.

* * * *

He'd made us a really delicious chicken salad, served with a chilled glass of Pinot Grigio. I thought as

I sat across from him at the small dining table that I perhaps hadn't spent a more pleasant two days in a long time. Apart from the altercation in the office. David's company made me feel mellow, as if all was right with the world. Which of course I knew to be far from the truth, but being with him, all that unpleasantness out there seemed to not be a part of our existence. Crazy, I knew, to be thinking in those terms already, but maybe after close to a year of being on my own, I was ready to settle again, give myself to a man I liked, if not yet loved. Of course, said man would have to want me too.

"Where are you, now?" David asked, gazing at me over the rim of his wineglass.

"I'm right here."

"Physically, yes, but mentally you were miles away. What is it that goes on in that mind of yours?"

"A load of rubbish, most of the time," I said, chuckling. "Rubbish that I think is important, but other people would find trivial self-indulgence."

"Jason." He leveled a hard look at me. "I haven't known you very long, but long enough I think to consider what you just said bullshit."

"How rude." I tried to maintain a lighthearted attitude, but he wasn't having it.

"Be serious."

"Must I?" I frowned at him. "Isn't life serious enough? Being with you makes me forget some of that, makes me wish I'd met you years ago, before..." I trailed off, not wanting to involve him in the shit story that was my life.

"Before what?" He reached over to hold my hand. "You can tell me, Jason. It might help you get over whatever it is that troubles you."

Oh, God...if only that were true.

"David, you are probably one of the nicest guys I've met in the past year or so. I'd like to get to know you better...a lot better, but there are some things best left unsaid."

"Like what?"

"Pushy..."

"You said you liked me pushy, but okay, if you'd rather not tell me, I understand."

I sighed. "And of course, it'll become the elephant in the room whenever we're together. Okay, I'll give you the *Reader's Digest* version to make it more palatable, to me, at any rate."

He squeezed my hand. "Only if you want to."

I don't want to. "I want to." I took a deep breath. "A few years ago, I met a guy, Darren by name, and I fell in love with him, like big-time falling in love. He was everything to me, and I, in my naïve fashion, thought he loved me in the same way. We were together for three years, and never in that time did I have cause to doubt that. Right until the last day we were together."

I paused to take a swig of the very fine white wine in my glass. "I was going on a convention for four days. The night before I left, he made love to me like it was going out of style. I couldn't get a hold of him the entire four days, and when I came back he was gone and the apartment was empty. No note, no voicemail message, nothing."

David was staring at me, an odd, angry expression on his face. "My God," he muttered. "What a complete asshole. What excuse did he give when you finally spoke to him?"

"I've never spoken to him. He wouldn't return my calls and when I tried to reach him at his office, I was told my calls would no longer be accepted."

"And you've never seen him in town? San Diego's not that large a city."

"Well, for a long time I wasn't going anywhere. Not to bars or even a night out with friends. My boss got irritated with me, said my colleagues were tired of my shitty attitude, that kind of thing. So I tried pulling myself together, called a friend I hadn't seen in ages. We went out...and you may not want to hear this, but I got a bit drunkie the first time and the bartender took me home and... Well, need I say more?"

He smiled. "Did it help?"

"It did, for a while, then a few weeks ago, I was out with a couple of friends and who walks into the fucking bar? Darren. If I thought I was over him, I was wrong. If I thought we'd one day get together again, I was even more wrong. The look on his face said it all. I was less than dirt under his shoes."

"Jason, cut that out," David snapped. "Not having you in his life is his loss, not yours. You deserve so much better than him. I don't even know the guy, but I hate him right now."

I nodded. "Thanks for that. And you know something? This is the first time I've told the story without dissolving into a weeping wreck. I think I have you to thank for that too."

He got up and held out his hand to me. When I took it he helped me off my chair. "Finish your wine," he said huskily. "When you're through I'm taking you back to bed and I'm gonna make love to you like you've never been made love to before. Okay?"

I finished that wine so damned fast it was amazing I didn't choke to death on it.

Chapter Sixteen

We spent the weekend together. I ran back to my place to get a change of clothes, my razor, comb and toothbrush. Saturday, we went to one of those movie houses where they serve food and drink right there at the seats in the auditorium. Sunday, we took a picnic lunch to Balboa Park then back at David's apartment, he made a pasta dish. In between all that eating we, as David called it, made love…over and over. I began to wonder at my stamina, but David was a few years older than me, and he didn't seem to be having any problems at all.

On the Sunday night we were lying in bed after making love, twice, when David said, "Can I ask you something?"

I gazed into his eyes and smiled. "Yes, I'll marry you."

"What?" He looked startled and I couldn't blame him.

"I was joking, David."

"Well…" He poked me in the ribs. "You shouldn't joke about things like that. I may decide to ask you one day, and what if I'm only joking?"

"Sorry." I kissed him and looked suitably chastened. "You wouldn't do that, would you? Joke about it I mean."

"Let me think about that." He chuckled, leaned over me and began sucking on my left nipple. I writhed under him and reached for his cock which I'd felt growing hard against my thigh.

Best weekend ever.

* * * *

During the week, I called Hector and gave him my apologies about not being available on the date he'd requested. He sounded disappointed but said he understood and maybe another time perhaps. I didn't want to tell him I had no intentions of being on hand as an escort anymore. I figured the best way to do that was to inform Noah so that he wouldn't recommend me to any of his clients in the future. I'd come to this decision after my weekend with David. It might have been a little early to regard David as my 'boyfriend'. We hadn't discussed it and I didn't want to jump the gun, as they say, but what I felt for David was something more than mere friendship.

There was a definite tingling inside me when I thought about him, and I thought about him a lot, even when under pressure to get a project done at work. That, and the fact we'd seen each other every night since our weekend together seemed to me a good indication that he was interested in our friendship progressing. But I was wary. After my experience with Darren I'd have been a fool not to have at least a few misgivings. Not that David gave off any negative signs. He was wonderful to be with, so warm and affectionate, funny and charming and absolutely dynamite in bed. I could get a hard-on just remembering the way he kissed me, smiled at me, held my hand. Yep, I was a goner all right, but it was way too soon to tell him. I so did not want to muck this up.

Of course I had to deal with William and Human Resources over my fracas with sullen John the Bigot. As I expected, William was not happy with me, and HR took a dim view of fisticuffs in the office, at dawn or any other time of day. I was reprimanded by the head of HR, a jolly plump lady who I think thought I was marvelous, but didn't dare say so. William sat watching us both with a faux stern expression. He clapped me on the shoulder after we'd left the HR office.

"I shouldn't say this, but I was hoping they'd terminate John. Save us all a lot of headaches, but they're only giving him a written warning, which will probably make him seethe, but that's his problem."

"As long as he cuts out the homophobic remarks, I don't give a crap where he is or what he does. I think not getting Phil's support kinda shocked him, so maybe that and the warning will make a better man of him." We both snorted with laughter as we got on the elevator to our department. Not nice, I know.

Toward the end of the week, Eric called me on my cell while I was on my way over to David's apartment to spend the evening with him. We were both hooked on the *Outlander* series after binge watching the first season and he'd just received the DVD of Season Two from Amazon.

"Hi, Eric, what's up?"

"Are you busy tonight?"

"Yeah, sorry. On my way to a friend's place. Is something wrong?"

"Yes. I'm being a bit of an idiot, I expect."

"Tell me about it."

"It's Steve, of course. Is it okay if I tell you we had sex?"

I suppressed the chuckle that threatened to escape my lips. "Of course, if you're comfortable talking about it."

"I don't have anyone else I can talk to about it, Jason. You're like my sex mentor."

I did laugh a little at that. "I think that's a compliment. Okay, what happened?"

"It was amazing, Jason. Totally amazing."

"Well, that's great. I'm happy for you." *So what the fuck's the problem?*

"Thing is, I haven't heard from him all week. He hasn't returned any of my texts or calls. I guess he just considers it a one-night stand…well, two, because we has sex two nights. Shit, Jason, I was starting to have feelings for him. Not that I thought he wanted to spend the rest of his life with me, but maybe just a bit longer than two nights."

Well, damn. This isn't unusual, but the fucker could at least have let him down gently. Shithead Steve. I'll have something to say to him when I see him at the bar next time.

"I'm sorry, Eric, but best you know now he's a waste of space rather than if you'd really gotten involved with him."

"I guess."

He sounded so down I wished I could comfort him by being there, but canceling my date with David was not something I was about to do. Still, I felt I had to do something. "Are you free for lunch tomorrow?"

194

"Name the place, I'll be there."

"How about Sal's Pizzeria on Fifth? I can be there at one."

"That'd be great, Jason. Sorry I'm being such a dork about this. It's just that…oh shit, I guess I'm just hurt he wasn't more interested in seeing me again."

"His loss," I told him. "Okay, gotta go, Eric. I'm outside my friend's place. See you tomorrow…and try not to think this is your fault. You're a gorgeous guy and you'll meet someone else and forget all about Steve."

"From your lips, as they say. See you, Jason, and thanks."

I hung up and felt bad for him. I knew he was going to think he shouldn't have bothered in the first place. I was just glad he didn't blame me for pushing him at Steve. But I hadn't really, had I? They were two hot guys, and in my opinion kinda belonged together. What in hell was Steve thinking, if he was thinking at all? Maybe I'd get his phone number from Matt and ask him point blank. Or was that me being way too pushy again?

I'd suggested lunch because I knew David also had midday plans with a couple of out-of-town clients. I was okay with that because I knew his clients were nothing like Noah's. He hadn't looked too happy when he'd told me about the meeting, saying he'd of course much rather spend the whole day with me. And the feeling was mutual, but it did give me time to soothe Eric's fragile ego…and besides, I liked the guy and it would be kinda nice to see him again.

* * * *

I'd thought it a good idea to tell David of my lunch plans because, well, it could happen that word of my being seen in the company of some hot dude would get back to him. So far, we didn't have any mutual friends, but better to be careful.

Eric was waiting for me when I got to the restaurant and apart from being down-in-the-dumps, he looked amazing as ever. He was wearing a blue denim shirt and jeans and with his cowboy boots adding even more to his height, he was a joy to behold.

"Hi." He wrapped me up in a big hug. "Thanks for doing this. I know this isn't part of your job."

"I don't have that job anymore, Eric. This is just you and me, friends, out together for lunch."

He stared at me for a moment, and I couldn't figure out what his reaction was. "Are you surprised?" I asked as we sat at a table on the patio.

"Kind of. You're so good at it. I was going to ask if I could come see you again...you know, like we did before."

"No, Eric. That's over, but we can be buddies, if you want."

He nodded. "Okay."

At my suggestion we ordered a pizza to share and house salads. I wasn't sure how to broach the subject of Steve in the conversation, but I didn't have to worry as Eric did the broaching.

"I called him again this morning," he said sadly, "but he didn't respond."

"What an ass-hat," I growled. "I hate it when someone just breaks off communication without an explanation." *Oh, boy, do I ever hate that.* 'Did you get any indication he was uninterested, or unhappy when he was with you?"

"No! The opposite. Last time he was over, he couldn't have been more loving, and kept telling me I was amazing, and gorg…well, that just sounds like I'm bragging, but he was so sweet, Jason. We had a great time, and I really thought he meant it."

Just as I thought Darren meant everything he said to me. Goddammit. Eric deserves so much better than this.

"You deserve better, Eric. And you'll find someone who'll love you and treat you with respect."

Our pizzas and salads arrived and I was glad to see Eric's depression hadn't curtailed his appetite. He fairly wolfed it all down in a matter of minutes and I smiled as I couldn't help but see Darren's expression of horror if we'd been sitting in one of his favorite over-priced and really not very terrific restaurants.

Eric wiped his mouth with his napkin then gazed at me expectantly. "What about you, Jason? You have a boyfriend?"

"Uh huh. We're kinda new, so no great expectations yet." That was a white lie. I had expectations all right. I just wasn't about to voice them at the moment.

"Have you had your heart broken?"

There was such a plaintive tone to his voice that I reached over and covered his hand with mine. "I'm still in recovery mode," I told him. "Eric, your heart isn't broken. You're hurt and that's understandable, but being dum…I mean set aside after two nights of hot sex does not constitute a reason for your heart to be broken. Try three years of thinking you were with your one and only then being left with an empty apartment, without a word of explanation. "

"That was you? Shit, I'm sorry, Jason, making you listen to my crap when you've been through something so terrible. I don't think I could handle that."

"Well, I've discovered it's not the end of the world, even if it seems so at the beginning. Like I said I'm in recovery mode, I'm doing okay, and I've met a really nice guy. And that's what I want for you. So don't give up just because some dopey bartender has given you the bum's rush."

He chuckled, his beautiful eyes gleaming with humor. "Dopey bartender! That's hilarious."

"I'm glad I could make you laugh. Why don't we go over to Bobby's Tavern and make out in front of him?"

He snorted with surprise. "You think that would make him laugh?"

"That's not the intention, Eric. It's to make him mad and have him leap over the bar to punch me on the nose!"

"*What?*"

"Don't worry. I'm quick on my feet and can run really fast."

Now he was laughing and I hoped it would help heal some of the hurt he was feeling. He wouldn't go to Bobby's with me, but after we parted company with a promise to keep in touch, I marched over there, determined to give dopey Steve a piece of my mind. As luck would have it, the bar wasn't particularly busy when I got there and Steve was shooting the breeze with the only two customers I could see. I waited until he turned to look at me, and the slow recognition on his face was worth the trip. I could tell he had just mentally said, '*Oh, fuck*'.

"What'll it be?" he asked, a semblance of a smile somewhere on his lips.

"Stella, draft, please," I said pleasantly enough. I watched as he worked the lever pouring my beer. He had a nice profile, nice hair, nice ass, nice everything really. Too bad he was such a skunk. "So, how've you been, Steve?"

"Okay. Not much going on, really."

I waited until he placed my beer in front of me. "So, how come you dumped my friend, Eric?"

"What?" He looked like I'd smacked him on the head.

"Eric. The tall, blond and beautiful guy I introduced you to. Why'd you dump him?"

"I didn't...I mean, he's uh...oh shit..." He pulled himself up and glared at me. "What's it gotta do with you, anyway?"

"He's my friend and I introduced him to you and you hit on him right away. So now I feel responsible for the world of hurt he's living in. That's what it's got to do with me."

"He's hurting?" His voice went up an octave on the last syllable.

"What d'you expect when the sweet guy he thought you were suddenly won't return a call or a text and he's left wondering what he did wrong."

"He didn't do anything wrong. It's me..."

"Oh, not the old 'it isn't you, it's me' syndrome, surely," I sneered.

"No, I mean it!" He flushed and glanced around then lowered his voice and leaned closer to me over the bar. "Listen, Eric is amazing, but have you been to his place? Do you know what he does, the kind of people he knows? He moves on a higher plane of existence than me, or maybe even you. Maybe not you 'cause you're his friend."

"What are you babbling about?"

"His folks are *billionaires*. I saw pictures of them in his penthouse... They're *famous*, for fuck's sake."

"And because of that you dumped him?" I stared at him, stupefied.

"He deserves someone so much better than me."

I couldn't help but notice his eyes, his very nice gray eyes, were glistening. Maybe he wasn't the skunk I'd just labeled him.

"Someone from his own social sphere," he continued, choking a little. "I couldn't even pretend to keep up with him or them. I'm a bartender. They'd think I was on the make, trying to con him or something."

"Don't you think you should let Eric make the decision as to whether you and he are compatible? You're a bartender now, but you're gonna be an environmental engineer. He was so excited when he told me that about you."

"He was?"

"Yes, dummy. Okay, I probably shouldn't tell you this, but he's crazy about you, Steve. He misses you and wants to see you and…well, you can figure out the rest. So call him, why don't you. Call him and say you are so, so sorry for not answering his calls sooner. Tell him you're a dope. He'll understand."

I swallowed the rest of my beer and put my glass down. "I must be on my way," I told him grandly. "Call him. Oh, and one more thing…" I fixed him with a steely glare. "I was never here."

I sloped off laughing quietly to myself and hoping like hell I'd done the right thing.

David was waiting for me when I made it over to his place. After a lot of long and thrilling kisses and me getting lost, and very hard, in his embrace he steered me over to the couch where we sat with our arms around each other.

"How was your lunch date?" he asked while kissing my ear.

"Good. And your client meeting?"

"Boring but productive, so I shouldn't complain." He paused for a moment then said, "I was thinking we should take a trip, if you can get time off work."

"Oh yeah? Where were you thinking?"

"Up the coast, maybe. Santa Barbara for a long weekend. You know it?"

I nodded. "I was there a few years back."

"With shithead? Then maybe that's not such a good idea."

"No, not with shithead. With my mom and dad. I'm talking more than a few years, when I think about it. I was a teenager."

"So you wouldn't mind going there again?"

"I'd love to, but anywhere with you would be fine with me." I snuggled into his side. "When were you thinking of going?" He was quiet. Had he changed his mind already? "What's wrong?"

He smiled at me. "I was envisioning you as a teenager. Bet you were cute. You have pictures?"

I laughed. "Pervert."

"Hey, as long as you were eighteen…"

"And you'd have been twenty-two." I grinned at him. "Man, I think we'd have burned up the sheets if we'd met then."

He kissed me. "What say we go burn up the sheets, right now?"

"Thought you'd never ask. But I have to shower first and clean my teeth so I'm fresh as a daisy for you."

"I'll join you," he said, chuckling. "Then we can both be fresh as daisies."

I squeezed his biceps. "Nothin' daisy-like about you, lover."

He laughed and carried me into the bedroom where we undressed each other, sharing so many kisses and gropings we almost didn't make it to the shower. God, but he was amazing to be with. Just the sight of his broad back and muscular butt as he preceded me into the bathroom got me going. I'd been hard since I first arrived at his apartment. Being in his arms could do that for me in a flash. Now, as he held out his hand and drew me into the shower stall then enfolded me in his embrace as the hot water streamed down over us, I felt as if I'd come home. I didn't want to move, just stay there with his arms around me, my face pressed to his while he placed tender kisses on my throat and shoulders.

He caressed my back and my ass with his big hands and I melted against him. He slid his erection over mine, the friction of hard flesh on hard flesh making me see stars. When he pressed a finger inside me, I moaned and pushed back on the pressure until he reached my prostate and curled his finger over it. More stars, more moans turning into words demanding he fuck me right there, right now!

He dragged me out of the shower and rubbed a towel roughly over me while I attempted to do the same for him. We were laughing and kissing, and still damp, we stumbled into the bedroom where we fell upon the bed in a tangle of arms and legs and parted lips. The sex bordered on the frantic for reasons I could never rationally explain. It was as if a fever had gripped us, and I knew this wasn't just me feeling slightly out of control. David was kissing me and holding me so tightly I was gasping in his arms and into his mouth and it was glorious and I wanted it to never end.

"Jason," David breathed against my lips. "Oh, my God, Jason…"

I knew what he was on the edge of saying, because I was there with him in that moment when everything became clear, and I knew without a shadow of a doubt that I had fallen in love with him. Scary as that was, I wanted to yell it out loud, but instead I told him in a choked-out whisper, and although it might have seemed impossible he held me even more tightly than before. His voice was husky but his words, "I love you too, Jason," were perfectly pronounced. And just like that I knew he was the man who would unbreak my heart.

After some fumblings with lube and a condom, I got what I had demanded in the shower. David inside me, fucking me with long, deep strokes, and kissing me with more passion that I thought possible from any living human. I had smirked when Hank had compared Lewis to a god, but here I was, gazing up into my lover's eyes and placing him far above all other men. And telling him so with a rush of words that most likely he didn't understand at the time. Never mind, I was going to tell him lots more times in the future.

After the euphoria of our simultaneous orgasms had started to fade, so the doubt set in. Was this all too good all too soon? Were we rushing things? Was he going to regret saying he loved me, in the morning?

"What are you thinking about now?" he asked, leaning over me. He was running his fingers up and down the insides of my thighs. Very distracting and very sexy.

"You don't think we were hasty in saying the 'L' word?"

"I wasn't being hasty. I'm a great believer in love at first sight. I know a lot of people poo-poo it, but you're the only guy who ever got my engines revving at first glance. That day in the gym, I looked at you and wanted you, both carnally and for the long term. It pissed me off that you were with Matt that day. I was sure I could lure you into my bed after that promise of coffee or something stronger. Me being the something stronger of course."

I chuckled and poked him in the ribs. "You thought I was that easy?"

"Not at all, just that I was that good."

We laughed quietly together and I pulled him close. "So I'll say it again. I love you, David Farmer."

"And I love you, Jason Harrison, and I think I always will."

Chapter Seventeen

A couple of days later, Noah called me. Apparently, Simon had told him that I had turned down a request from Hector and that he'd been very disappointed, and had asked if it was something he'd done.

"Nothing like that, Noah," I told him. "As a matter of fact, I enjoyed my time with Hector. He's a very sweet man."

"What was the problem then?" he asked.

"No problem. I decided I didn't want to do the escorting thing anymore."

"And when were you going to tell me this?" His tone was decidedly frosty.

Jeez, he could get pissy so fast. Just as well we hadn't entered into anything other than a business relationship. There was a definite similarity to the way Darren would talk to me sometimes.

"Yeah, sorry. I was going to call you after Russ left a message saying he and a friend wanted to get together with me when they were in town. Must've slipped my mind. Of course, I wasn't about to agree to it without your okay."

"What's going on, Jason?"

"I met a guy, Noah. A sweet and stable guy that I've fallen in love with, and I don't want to screw things up by continuing to service men on the side. That never was me, really. I only did it to please you. I thought it would be exciting, and it was a couple of times. But it's not what I want anymore. I hope you understand."

"This guy...does he know you had a bad breakup and he might possibly be on the rebound?"

"He knows about Darren, yes. But he's not on the rebound, Noah. That's kind of a bitchy thing to infer."

"How long have you been seeing him?"

"Uh, not quite three weeks. I mean, I met him earlier, but we've only been seeing each other for about three weeks, but I know what I'm feeling for him is real."

"Strange," he said, the trace of sarcasm in his tone unmistakable. "Not so very long ago, you said you had feelings for me, and now a few short weeks later you're telling me you're in love with some other guy. Pardon me for thinking you might just be rushing into this relationship simply because you need someone in your life, because you're adrift, still pining for Darren – plus the fact that I didn't show enough interest."

I sucked in a deep breath rather than let loose with just what I thought of his arrogance. Maybe I should've let those bullies beat the crap out of him all those years ago. *That's not nice, Jason*, I reprimanded myself, but I'd had enough of this conversation.

"Um..." I reined in my anger sufficiently, but I wasn't going to let him get away with that crap altogether. "Let me just say this, Noah. I want to thank you for not showing enough interest. If you had then I might never have met David, the man I'm dating and with whom I am in love. There's no rebound, Noah. He is a wonderful man and—"

"And, what d'you think he'll say when he finds out you were a paid escort, even for the short amount of time you accepted money for your services?"

His sinister tone reverberated in my ears and I exploded. "Are you kidding me? You're *threatening* me, Noah? Oh, where is the sweet and sensitive man who's been fooling my parents for years? Just as well you're a hundred miles away, or—"

"I'm sorry…sorry, Jason. That was uncalled for. Of course, I wouldn't say anything to destroy your relationship." I heard him take a deep breath and let it out in a long, long sigh. "Truly sorry, Jason. I don't know what came over me. I guess I'm kicking myself for letting you find someone else. My fault, but don't blame me for feeling bitterness over my mistake."

"*Noah…*" Shit, now I felt bad.

"It's okay, Jason. I wish you every happiness. I don't want there to be any awkwardness should we meet again."

"There won't be."

"Good. Okay, I have to go. Bye, Jason, and lots of luck."

"Bye, Noah."

I stared at my cell for a long time after we'd hung up. That was quite the conversation. I hadn't ever imagined Noah confessing to having more than a passing interest in me. Perhaps if he'd been more upfront things would have been different. *But, be honest, Jason. Could you have endured a relationship with him knowing what he was doing while you were at work? And the answer would have to be a big fat no!*

207

One thing I knew for certain. I was not taking any chances of David finding out about my male escorting from anyone else but me. Perhaps there was no longer a threat from Noah. I felt pretty secure in thinking that his momentary lapse of refinement was more about anger at himself than at my falling for David. However, there were several other people involved who just might drop it into a conversation, either by intent or by accident. I couldn't have that happen. David had to hear it from me, and soon. Tonight, if I could summon the courage. *Fuck!*

I had arranged for David to meet Pete and Hank at Bobby's Tavern that night, and I was so tempted to cancel, but maybe with a couple of drinks under my belt, and David having a nice time meeting my friends—I was sure they'd love him—I could tell him all when we were on our own.

When we entered Bobby's, I immediately zeroed in on the tall blond guy sitting at the bar talking with Steve. *Eric.* Holy shit, Steve must've actually taken my advice and called him. I was going to avert my gaze, but Steve caught me looking and said something to Eric who turned and waved, a big smile on his face. I waved back but kept walking to where Pete and Hank waited for us at a table. I wasn't sure how I'd introduce Eric to David and for the life of me I couldn't remember the story I'd told Pete. He was somebody's nephew, right?

I introduced David to Pete and Hank and he seemed to be very relaxed with them. He bought a round then we all sat and the guys peppered David with questions that he answered with good humor. I looked up as Eric bounced in front of our table like a giant jack-in-the-box. God, but he was overdoing this happiness kick.

"Hi," he exclaimed, while Hank's mouth fell open at the sight of him. Pete looked delighted to see him again.

"Hi, Eric," I said. "This is my boyfriend, David." I tried not to put an emphasis on the word 'boyfriend', just wanted to give him a head's up in case he said something a little too personal. "And this is Hank. Hank and I work together."

"Great." He gave us all beaming smiles. "Can I join you for a few minutes? Steve got real busy over there all of a sudden."

"Of course."

He pulled up a chair next to Hank who was still staring at him like he was a Norse god or something.

"So you're seeing Steve?" Pete asked.

"Yes, we're dating as of two days ago, thanks to Jason."

Oh shit, here we go. David glanced at me with interest. "What did you do? Play the fairy godmother?"

"Please." I gave him a disparaging look. "No fairies at this table."

Eric laughed. He was fairly brimming with *joie de vivre.* "Jason introduced us, then when Steve didn't call, Jason came over here and read him the riot act. Told him he was a dope if he didn't call me. Anyway, everything's good now."

"I'm glad to hear it," I said, meaning it. "You guys look great together."

Steve showed up on his break and hung over Eric's shoulders, kissing his face before suggesting they find a spot together, alone. After they left, Hank asked, "How do you know Eric?"

Shut up, Hank. "Uh, he's the uh nephew of a friend of mine."

"I thought he was the nephew of your folks' friends," Pete remarked.

"Uh, yeah, that's right."

David glanced at me, but didn't say anything and I was glad when Hank went on about how stunning Eric was and I had to remind him he was already seeing a stunning someone and to quit flirting with every good-looking guy that stopped at our table. All in jest of course.

I was right about one thing. Pete and Hank loved David. In fact, I had to keep my eye on Pete, who kept giving David way-too-long looks and once or twice I caught him licking his lips while looking. *Oh, no you don't, you vixen, he's mine!*

We'd had a good evening and I hugged David's arm to my side as we walked to his car.

"Your place or mine?" he asked, grinning at me.

"Let's go to mine." That way, I thought deviously, if he got mad after I told and stormed out he had a car to burn rubber in. If we went to his place and he got mad, I'd be walking home…and it was miles!

Once in my apartment I was more on edge than ever. "Like a drink?" I asked.

"Better not. I have to drive home."

"You can stay."

"Can't. I have a seven o'clock breakfast meeting and it's suit and tie."

"Poor you."

"What's wrong, Jason? You seem nervous."

"Can't fool you, can I?" I grabbed a glass and sloshed some Scotch into it then took a giant swallow.

"*Jason*, what's wrong?" He was staring at me with those excellent eyebrows of his near his hairline.

"Oh, God, David, I don't know how to tell you this."

He paled. "You're breaking up with me?"

"No! Jesus, no!"

"Okay then." He appeared to relax, smile even. "I'd have thought it crazy as you must have told me you love me at least nine times today."

"Only nine?" I said weakly.

He took me in his arms. "C'mon, spill. What can be so bad that you can't tell me?"

Oh shit, if you only knew. What am I saying? You're gonna know... I cleared my throat and stepped out of his embrace. I didn't really think he'd take a swing at me, but a couple of feet away seemed like a safe distance in case he imploded.

"Uh, a couple of months ago I went to my dad's birthday party...his sixty-sixth birthday." For some reason I thought that bit of information important. Fuck knows why. "I met this guy, Noah, that I went to school with years ago. He said his name and I couldn't believe it. He'd been this short, fat asthmatic kid, and now he was tall, beautiful and elegant, and I have to admit I was attracted to him. We went out to dinner the following night and we had sex afterward."

I paused long enough to dare a glance at David's expression. He was just looking back at me, without any discernable dismay. Then again, why would he? This was before I'd met him. "Anyway," I continued when he didn't say anything, "Noah told me he was a male escort and rented himself out by the hour. Of course, ha ha, he didn't charge me for our time together."

"I should hope not," David said. "He should've been paying *you*."

Oh, God. "Funny you should say that, because he asked me if I'd accompany a client of his to dinner, here in town. No sex, he assured me, and there wasn't, David. Even on the second night when Simon asked me to go to a party with him, there was not a mention of me going back to the hotel with him. He was a really nice man, but he did pay me for my time. Then…"

I stopped and took a deep breath. "A friend of Simon's called me and…"

David nodded. "I think I know where this is going."

"Yes, but let me tell you so it's all out in the open and I don't have to worry about you hearing it from someone else. It wasn't bad, David. The guy was sweet really. Shy and inexperienced and I…well, I gave him what he wanted, and he paid me."

"How many men, Jason?"

"Not many, and none of it was gross. I have to admit when Noah told me what he did I was kinda shocked, but more from the image of him having sex with some dirty old men, but it wasn't like that really…"

I stumbled to a halt and tears welled in my eyes. "David, please believe me, if I'd known I was going to meet you and fall in love with you, I never would have agreed to any of it, even for Noah. I love you so much, and I don't want this to ruin what we have."

He studied me for so long that I thought any minute he was going to turn and leave without a word. "Can I ask a question?" he finally said.

"Of course, anything."

"Have you serviced anyone since you and I…well, since we've been seeing each other?"

"No…I wouldn't do that. I couldn't. Meeting you was my one big hope that you'd be the one who…" I couldn't stop the tears that slipped from my eyes. If he was going to leave me now, to break my heart so soon after putting it together, I just didn't know what I'd do.

But I deserved it, didn't I? I'd been a whore, and David...he was so good, so true.

"I have another question."

Oh, God. "Yes, David?"

"The guy we met tonight, the tall blond...Eric. I didn't buy the nephew story. Was he one of your clients?"

"Well, he actually is the nephew of, uh, this guy I know...knew rather, who was, *is* his uncle. And yes, I was asked to...to, uh, *help* him, because he'd just come out to his uncle and told him he'd never been with a man, so..."

"Well, it looks like you succeeded." There was no rancor in his tone which surprised and pleased me. "He certainly came across as a happy camper with the bartender."

"Yes..." But I still had to make him forgive me. I swiped at the tears with the back of my hand. "David, I would give anything to make all of this not happen...I mean all of what I was doing before I met you. I'm sorry, David, if you think differently about me, but I'll understand if you want to dump me. I don't deserve you, I know I don't."

He stepped toward me and took me in his arms and I was near to collapse, sobbing like a teenage girl who'd just found out her first beau has been screwing the football quarterback.

"Hush, Jason. I'm not going to *dump* you as you so elegantly put it. I'd be a complete self-righteous idiot if I walked out on you for this. A few years ago, I was fucking anything in pants that moved. We all have a past, Jason."

"But you didn't charge them for it," I moaned.

"No, I didn't think of it at the time. More fool me."

I barked out something that was both a sob and a laugh. *Jesus, what a strange noise.* "Sorry, that was a hideous sound."

He laughed quietly and kissed my soggy cheeks. "Maybe I will stay over tonight. You need some loving, and I promise there won't be a bill on the nightstand when I leave in the morning."

I gaped at him. Was there ever a man as wonderful as him? I dropped my head onto his shoulder and nuzzled the crook of his neck. "I love you, David, with my whole heart and soul."

"Good, 'cause I'd be really pissed if it was all on my side." He patted my butt. "Now, let's hit the sheets, and see how hot we can make 'em. Like that idea?"

"Love it. No better idea in the whole wide world."

Epilogue

Three months later

"I guess that's it," I said, running a length of Scotch tape over the last box I'd packed. David, at my side, hefted the box into his arms then made for the door.

"Come on then." He was halfway down the stairs before I caught up with him. I was excited. This was my official 'moving in with David' day. The escrow on his new condo had finally closed last week and he'd taken me out to dinner to celebrate then popped the question. No, not *that* question.

"Would you like to move in with me?" had been the question.

Would I? Of course I would. We spent almost every day and night in each other's company as it was, so splitting a monthly payment seemed like a sensible idea. That, and the fact we got along so well made us ignore the warnings from well-meaning, but pain-in-the-ass friends who'd muttered things like, *'too soon'*, *'shouldn't you think about it?', 'what if you have a falling-out?'* etcetera, etcetera.

"What if we have a falling out?" I'd said to David after listening to one of those warnings.

"What?" He'd looked at me blankly.

"A falling out. People do have them."

"Why would we have one?"

"Because…" I couldn't really think of a reason, except that I could be a bit of a slob on occasion while David was a bit of a neatnik, all the time. "Well, you know what a pain I can be at times, not picking up after myself…and you, you're Mister Clean!"

He'd laughed. "If that's all you've got I don't think it'll lead to a 'falling out'. If you get too sloppy I'll just put you over my knee and spank you."

I'd grinned at him. "Spank me now then I'll know what's in store."

So I said goodbye to my little North Park apartment and hello to David's ultra-new condo with its view of the glittering pool below and the tops of the tall buildings downtown. David had arranged a little get-together of friends for a kind of house warming. Fortunately he'd ordered trays of food to be delivered from Whole Foods so that neither one of us would be stuck in the kitchen. As I was a bit of a disaster in that corner of the condo, I was hugely relieved to hear it.

He'd invited my mom and dad. Three weeks ago I had dragged him up to Sherman Oaks to meet them. Not dragged, he'd come most willingly. I knew they'd love him, and I was right. He and my dad hit it off immediately, retiring to Dad's favorite spot on the patio, beers in hand, talking like old friends.

Mom was lavish in her praise. How could she not be, considering she had never liked Darren and had only put up with him for my sake? She had never been rude or critical to his face, unlike Darren's parents who could be downright hostile at times. David was probably the polar opposite of Darren, and sometimes I would marvel at my luck in finding him. What were the words to that old song?

Somewhere in my youth or childhood, I must have done something good.

That had to be it, but I had a hard time coming up with the 'good' I must have done.

"Funny," Mom was saying and I snapped myself out of my day-dreaming to pay attention. "Your dad and I thought you and Noah might hit it off. You seemed so happy to see him after all these years."

"Oh, yeah, it was good seeing him, but he and I have different interests. He's more of…uh, a social animal than I am."

Mom laughed. "What silliness, dear. You're both young and gay. You should have the same interests, surely."

"Uh, well, not all gay guys have the same interests, just like all straight guys differ. Some like football, some like baseball…that kind of thing. And some gay guys don't like musicals, or Lady Gaga."

"You're rambling, Jason," Mom said. "Well, your David is a lovely man and I can tell from the way he looks at you that he's head over heels. Something I never saw when Darren was with you. You're well shot of him."

I couldn't deny that. There had been a time in my life when I thought I'd never get over the loss of Darren in my life. Now I could look back on that time as far too many wasted months. Months of my life I'd never get back, and I wasn't going to waste one minute of one hour thinking about him ever again.

* * * *

After stowing my boxes in the spare room till I got around to unpacking, we showered, fooled around in the shower, loved each other on the bed then got dressed and ready to meet our guests. David had invited a couple of people from his office, Penny and Martin, who arrived together and I naturally thought they were an item.

"No," David whispered in my ear. "Penny's a lesbian and Martin's even shyer than I am."

I slapped his arm playfully. "There's not a shy bone in your body. I hope you don't mind that I invited Eric and Steve. They seem so happy together, don't they?" Of course I had cleared it with him ahead of time, but I just wanted to be sure he was okay with it, knowing Eric's and my history.

"Of course, I don't. And yes, they do look happy." He gave me an evil smile. "I guess your lessons paid off, for both of them." I slapped his arm again, this time less playfully. We were *not* going there....ever.

The other guests, Mom and Dad, Hank and Lewis, William and his wife Mary, Pete and Maggie – a girlfriend of his as he hadn't managed to snag a new boyfriend yet – were a good mix and the living room was filled with the sounds of conversation and laughter, along with the clinking of glasses.

I hadn't invited Noah. That might have just been too much, although maybe it would have done him good to spend an evening among people he wasn't expected to have sex with when the party was over. I was sure that one day our paths would cross again and I could introduce David to him and he could see for himself how my luck had changed so much for the better.

David brought me a drink and stood with me, his arm around my waist. "Happy?" he asked.

"Completely, totally and absolutely," I told him and gave him a quick kiss on his smoothly shaven cheek. Mom crossed the living room to join us.

"Such a handsome pair you make," she said.

"You wouldn't be a teeny bit biased, would you?" I teased her.

"Not at all, although I do think the standout here is Eric....oh, and Lewis. Both so tall and heroic looking. It's been a long time since I was in a room filled with so much eye-candy."

David snorted out a laugh and I said, "Mom, where'd you learn that expression?"

"Oh, I think I heard it on *The Bachelor* or maybe at one of my ladies' groups. We do notice these things, you know." She looked up at David and smiled. "I am so glad my son met you. I think I can stop worrying about him now."

I rolled my eyes to heaven, but David bent to give her a gentle kiss on her cheek. "I'm glad I met him too, Marjory, and I promise to make sure he stays out of trouble."

"Hey." I raised my hand to slap his arm again, but he grabbed my wrist and laid his lips on my palm. *In front of my mother.*

"Oh, how sweet," she crooned.

Ah, to love and be loved...is there anything more wondrous?

Want to see more from this author?
Here's a taster for you to enjoy!

The Love Between Us
J.P. Bowie

Excerpt

From his position behind the bar at Bobby's Tavern, Matt Johnson surveyed the crowd that filled almost every square inch of the largest gay bar in San Diego. He sighed. Another night of forcing a smile to his lips and thinking of something humorous to pass on to the customers who got tipsier, and sometimes downright drunkier, with every passing hour.

It wasn't as if he didn't like his job—he did—but in the past few months, he'd felt as if, somehow, he'd been left behind. Not sexually, for sure. He had more than his fair share of guys wanting to spend time with a hot bartender. Matt knew he was hot—he'd been told so many, many times—but, it seemed, not hot enough to keep a guy interested for more than a few nights. He was still young, he'd told himself a hundred times. There were still a lot of years ahead for him to find the 'one', weren't there?

It was just that in the four years he'd been working at Bobby's Tavern, almost everyone he'd known, whether they worked together or were friends he'd see on his nights off, had somehow managed to get themselves seriously involved with another guy. So, why couldn't he? Was he regarded as that much of a flake? He'd overheard a remark like that a few months ago, from someone who thought he knew him, and Matt had wanted to turn around and say, "You don't know me at all." But he hadn't said it, couldn't really, because the man was a customer, and rudeness from the bar staff was not allowed at Bobby's Tavern.

Jack Felton, the owner and manager, had fired a couple of bartenders for just that offense, and if there was something Matt needed badly, it was to keep this job. Nowhere else, without a college degree, could he earn the kind of money he did here. Steve, his relief bartender, was studying to be an environmental engineer. Well, good luck to him, but he was going to miss the tips that didn't come with a job like that. Still, he did have that hunk of a wealthy boyfriend he was living with should things not pan out for him.

Matt sighed again then had to quickly jump to it as Brett, the other bartender on duty, looked like he was getting swamped with orders all of a sudden.

"What'll it be?" he asked a cute, fresh-faced blond kid who yelled his order over the combined din of voices and music that was a nightly staple at Bobby's.

"Two screwdrivers and a Stella."

Is this kid twenty-one? "You have ID?"

The 'kid' laughed, his gaze settling on Matt's bare chest. "I'm twenty-three, but thanks for the compliment." He handed over his driver's license without hesitation.

Matt smiled after he'd glanced at it. "You must get that a lot…Taylor."

"I do…uh, what's your name?"

"Matt."

"Nice to meet you, Matt. Anyway, I get asked for ID nearly every time in bars me and my buds don't go to a lot. We live in LA and usually go to Sykes on Melrose. They know us there." He waved a hand behind him to include the two guys standing there. Both looked to be the same age as Taylor.

"Well, enjoy your evening," Matt said while he fixed their drinks.

"We're here for the weekend, so we'll most likely come here again." Taylor gave him a flirty smile. "Are you working tomorrow night?"

Matt nodded and passed Taylor the two screwdrivers. "The Stella for you?"

"Yes." Taylor turned to hand over the screwdrivers to his friends. When he turned back to face Matt, he asked, "What time d'you get off tonight?"

"Not till two a.m., sorry." He watched the frown of disappointment crease Taylor's forehead. "But I'm off at nine tomorrow night if you're thinking of buying me a drink."

Taylor's expression lightened. "That, and anything else you'd like."

"It's a date. That'll be fifteen for the screwdrivers. Your beer's on the house."

"Thanks." He slipped Matt a twenty. "Keep the change."

"Lose your friends tomorrow night. They won't be hurt, will they?"

"They're married, so, no." Taylor grinned at him. "They'll be in bed by nine." He stepped out of the way to let another couple of customers reach the bar. "See you later, Matt."

He should have felt better about scoring with the cute guy, but if the truth be told, Matt was getting tired of the one-night stands, tired of the indifference after the second or third night. He'd always said he was happy to be some guy's fuck buddy, happy for there to be no real commitment, just good times. If the sex was really good, then so much the better. But recently it had definitely palled when he thought about what some people he knew had…the same man in their bed every night, and delight with the status quo.

Taylor came back to the bar, three or four more times, his smile of anticipation always in place. *Seems like a nice guy*, Matt thought. *Too bad he lives in LA, land of the parking lot freeways.* Toward the end of the evening, he scanned the thinning crowd to see if Taylor had hung around, but there was no sign of him or his friends. *That's okay, I'm bushed anyway.* Friday and Saturday nights were always a bear, but the tips made it all worthwhile.

On his way home, he stopped in at Fawkes, an all-night café a few blocks from his apartment. Not the chicest place in town, but the burgers were to die for, and Matt was starving. While he waited for his burger to go, Matt stared out of the window at the late-night stragglers wending their ways either home or to a local hotel. Mostly guys, their arms around each other probably for support, he reckoned, rather than affection, although it could have been a combination of the two.

Anyway, it's more than I have right now. Okay, he had to stop with the self-pity. It wasn't attractive and nobody had the patience to listen to a whiner. Nobody he knew, at any rate.

"Here you go, Matt," Al, the guy in charge at night said. "I put some fries on the side even though you didn't ask for 'em." He stared at Matt's flat stomach. "You gotta lotta room for 'em, by the looks of you."

"Thanks, Al." He'd been coming to Fawkes off and on for the last couple of years, so he knew better than to argue about the fries. He didn't have to eat them when he got home. Tonight, he just might. Burger, fries and a beer. *Better than… Nah, not really.*

Working at Bobby's, he was able to afford a nice apartment. *As nice as Jason's, anyway*, he thought, looking around at the cozy living room. But Jason had moved into that fancy place with David, the guy he'd met at the gym. *Stole him right from under my nose.* Not really, but it had rankled for a bit. He and Jason had been fuck buddies, although if he were being honest with himself, he wished he'd asked for more. He didn't see Jason often these days, like he used to. Guys who got serious usually didn't make a habit of frequenting gay bars, apart from getting together with friends occasionally. Matt guessed he could understand that. Once a guy was hooked, there wasn't that pressing need to go out and mingle with other 'desperately seeking someones'.

Man, but he was getting jaundiced in his opinions. When had that happened? He wasn't desperate…he had his share of the good life. And tomorrow night there'd be one more slice — Taylor, all hot and ready to get fucked before he had to go back to La-la land.

He stripped, threw his clothes in the laundry basket then slipped on a pair of shorts and, after getting a can of beer from the fridge, prepared to devour the burger and fries. He turned on the television, mainly to fill the room with sound instead of the silence that seemed to pervade the space on the nights he came home alone.

But I'm not lonely…not really. I have friends. Brett and Steve at Bobby's…Jason. Yes, he's still a friend of mine. We were real close there for a while until…but I still see him now and then, don't I? When he comes in with his buddies, he always stops and says hello.

"Fuck it." He stood and walked into the kitchen to dump the burger wrappers and get himself another beer. Truth was, he missed the times he'd spent with Jason. He'd been so sweet in bed. Sweet and kinda rough sometimes. He'd liked to mix it up. Matt had liked that too, but Jason had never made him feel he was just there for the sex. Afterward they'd cuddled and talked…almost like boyfriends.

There had been others since then, maybe too many others, and none of them had made him feel like Jason had. Well, he'd messed up for sure, letting him slip away like that without telling him, without saying the words that might have kept him by Matt's side.

"I love you." Yeah, those were the words. The words he hadn't said, had never said to another guy…and now it was too late. Jason and David had been living together now for six months, and from what he'd heard it didn't sound like they were having any problems or regrets. Not that he'd wish them to have. *I'm not that fucking desperate…*

* * * *

Saturday night and the place was jumping. It was difficult to tell which was louder—the clamor of the crowd or the blare of the pop-rock reverberating through the speakers. Another night when Matt would go home with his ears still ringing. Steve had called to say he was going to be late and hoped Matt didn't mind. Yes, Matt minded. He'd told Taylor he'd be off at nine, and he couldn't leave Brett on his own, not on a night like this. They'd even got the bar waiters mixing drinks to help them out.

"Fuckin' Steve," he growled under his breath. He was probably late because he was banging Eric through the mattress. He told himself he wasn't annoyed because he was jealous. He got plenty of action — and probably would tonight — but it irked him that Steve thought it was okay to call at the last minute and say he'd be late. He scanned the crowd to see if Taylor was already among the throng so he could tell him he'd be late getting off shift, but so far there was no sign of the cute blond.

For the next half-hour or so he was kept busy mixing drinks and pulling pints, and when Steve arrived and apologized again for being late, he was surprised to see it was already nine-thirty. And still no sign of Taylor. For a moment Matt couldn't believe the guy would be a no-show. That didn't happen very often. In fact, he couldn't remember the last time he'd been stood up. Maybe he'd got sick or run out of money and had to go home, or…he'd gotten lucky with someone else.

"So, are you leaving?" Steve asked. "Or are you so enamored of working here you wanna stay till closing time?"

"I'm leaving. How's Eric?" Matt scanned the crowd again — still no sign of his supposed date.

"Delightful as always," Steve said smugly. "I can't believe it's been nearly nine months already. We had dinner over at Jason and David's place last night. Jason said to tell you 'hi'."

"Did he?" Matt tried not to feel hurt. He really did, but it didn't work too well. Jason had never asked him over for dinner, but maybe that was David's decision. Most likely Jason had told him about their fuck-buddy days and the guy maybe thought he didn't need any more competition. Jason was a looker, and although

David was handsome and all, he was older and… *Christ, I am being such a prick right now.*

"You okay?" Steve squeezed Matt's shoulder. "You look like you're in pain."

"No, I'm okay. Just wonderin' if I'll go home or take in a movie. I've had enough of bars for the night."

Steve nodded. "Know what you mean. When I get off shift, I am so ready just to get home to my man." He flinched. "Yeah, sorry, Matt, didn't mean to sound smug." Matt had confided in Steve a while back that he and Jason had a sexual relationship and how he, Matt, had wished it could have been more. Steve had sympathized but hadn't come up with any advice, but by then of course, David had come along and that, as they say, was that.

Matt forced out a laugh. "Hey, some of us prefer to be single-o. No ball and chain for me, not yet anyway. Okay, I'll see you tomorrow…if you can pull yourself away from your *man.*"

He went into the back room to get his shirt and slip it on then walked through the bar, looking for any sign of the missing Taylor. By the time he got to the exit, he'd been groped about a dozen times. *Nothing like drunken queens to forget their manners.* He said hi to a couple of familiar faces then walked past the smokers outside and headed for his car and home.

PUBLISHING

Sign up for our newsletter and find out about all our romance book releases, eBook sales and promotions, sneak peeks and FREE romance books!

About the Author

J.P. Bowie was born in Scotland and toured British theatres in numerous musical shows including Stephen Sondheim's Company.

He emigrated to the States and worked in Las Vegas, Nevada for the magicians Siegfried and Roy as their Head of Wardrobe at the Mirage Hotel. He is currently living with his husband in sunny San Diego, California.

J.P. Bowie loves to hear from readers. You can find his contact information, website details and author profile page at https://www.pride-publishing.com

Lightning Source UK Ltd.
Milton Keynes UK
UKHW010634030920
369287UK00001B/93